JAX

The Mavericks, Book 3

Dale Mayer

Books in This Series:

Kerrick, Book 1
Griffin, Book 2
Jax, Book 3
Beau, Book 4
Asher, Book 5
Ryker, Book 6
Miles, Book 7
Nico, Book 8
Keane, Book 9
Lennox, Book 10
Gavin, Book 11
Shane, Book 12

JAX: THE MAVERICKS, BOOK 3
Dale Mayer
Valley Publishing Ltd.

Copyright © 2019

All rights reserved. Except for use in any review, the reproduction or utilization of this work in whole or in part by any electronic, mechanical or other means, now known or hereafter invented, including xerography, photocopying and recording, or in any information storage or retrieval system, is forbidden without the written permission of the publisher.

This is a work of fiction. Names, characters, places, brands, media, and incidents are either the product of the author's imagination or are used fictitiously. Any resemblance to actual events, locales, or persons, living or dead, is entirely coincidental.

ISBN-13: 978-1-773362-03-8
Print Edition

About This Book

What happens when the very men—trained to make the hard decisions—come up against the rules and regulations that hold them back from doing what needs to be done? They either stay and work within the constraints given to them or they walk away. Only now, for a select few, they have another option:

The Mavericks. A covert black ops team that steps up and break all the rules … but gets the job done.

Welcome to a new military romance series by *USA Today* best-selling author Dale Mayer. A series where you meet new friends and just might get to meet old ones too in this raw and compelling look at the men who keep us safe every day from the darkness where they operate—and live—in the shadows … until someone special helps them step into the light.

No time to rest. The world is a mess …

He'd barely made it home from helping Griffin only to find himself called to rescue a doctor on a cruise ship overtaken by pirates in their search for Abigail Dalton. The pirates had no trouble killing passengers until they found the right woman. With one man at his side, Jax sneaks onto the ship to rescue her.

When she heard the gunfire, Abby hid in the venting on the ship. When a man susses out her hiding place, she's sure her world is about to end. Only Jax is on her side; yet he came with just one man to help. Stunned, she stays close as

Jax frees the ship and keeps her safe—until they find out the real reason for this nightmare, when she's forced to England to face the two-legged monster of her nightmares ...

The safest place is at Jax's side, but Abby knows all too well how slippery this monster really is and how easily he steps from the shadows to grab his victims ...

CHAPTER 1

Jax Darrum had seen it coming, but he wondered how they would make it work. As far as he understood, Kerrick and Amanda were doing just fine in Paris. But Lorelei and Griffin? … Well, they had hit it off right from the beginning and Jax couldn't be happier for his friend. It was a lonely lifestyle these SEALs had chosen to lead, and each and every one of them had come to this point as a jumping off spot to something different, to making a choice to do something else.

He hadn't told Griffin but Jax's agreement to come on this mission was so that he could take the lead on one op and one op only. He was leaving the military, and he was leaving everything to do with this type of life. The Mavericks team had asked Jax specifically to help Griffin as a warm-up to doing his one mission sometime later. He figured that it was the same for Kerrick and for Griffin. Jax wasn't sure about joining the Mavericks unit for what would be his one big job, but the unit trained everybody before they took the lead on their one mission and then were done. But, as Jax thought about it, nobody in the Mavericks unit needed training.

This was like the peak of their careers for them. Jax didn't know if they would all be brought back to do something else. It was possible though, and Jax would consider it.

He also knew that most of them were getting paid enough money that they wouldn't have to work again. He'd never discussed that part either with Griffin or Kerrick. Jax didn't even know if Griffin knew what Kerrick had gone through. What Jax did know was that the next job was his to head up. He hoped that he had a couple weeks or a month or two before then. Hell, he'd be happy to have a year or two in between these particular jobs.

They were hard and intense, but once the op was done, so was he. He didn't have friends or family to worry about, so he was in a much easier situation than Griffin and Kerrick. Although, now that they had met and been partnered up for these Mavericks operations, things had changed for those guys too. That didn't mean that they, in any way, shape, or form, were ready to go out the same as Jax was. They'd all come to the point where, if this was the last mission for them, then that was the last mission, and they didn't really care to go on any more missions.

Neither did he. He was moving on to something different. He just didn't know what. He had a hankering for travel, to see the world as a tourist for a change, instead of skulking through the night in the shadows of darkness, watching other shadows move as they tried to take over worlds and governments and individuals.

Sitting on a beach and watching the sunrise would be a pretty decent way to spend his time, and sitting on the same damn beach and watching each new sunset would be a unique opportunity for him to just relax, maybe with a cold beer and with a friend or two. Now that would make his life pretty damn perfect.

He was headed back home again. He had been on his phone, setting up arrangements for his apartment and making sure his landlady knew he would arrive soon. The silly things in life that you had to organize. As he landed in California and grabbed his single bag and headed outside the airport, his cell buzzed.

He glanced down at the screen, groaned, and said, "Hell no. What?"

"How tired out are you?"

"Fucking tired," he said. "It's not like I got much sleep on the last job."

"That was two days ago," the man said in exasperation.

Jax heard something in that voice, and he asked, "Hell, Griffin, is that you?"

Griffin chuckled. "Hell yeah, it's me. Is that okay?"

"I don't know," Jax said. "What do you want?"

Immediately all the humor fled as Griffin said, "We need you."

"Are you coming with me?"

"No. Somebody will though."

"Why is it always like that?" he asked. "Some of these jobs are getting pretty thin for just one or two of us."

"If it can be more, it'll be more. I promise I won't send you out without backup."

He snorted at that. "But it won't be you though, right? You'll be holed up somewhere nice and cozy with Lorelei."

"If I could join you, I would," Griffin said regretfully. "Lorelei and I will see each other on a regular basis now, spending time with Amelia Rose too. We're giving the child time to adapt before Lorelei leaves."

"I'm almost jealous," Jax said. "*Almost* but not quite."

Griffin snorted. "Your time will come. You won't even see it happening, and, before you know it, it'll be right there in your face."

"I doubt it," he said, "but whatever. So, what's the job?"

Griffin took a long, slow breath and said, "You won't like it."

"I never liked any of 'em," he said. "So what's the deal?"

"We've got a cruise ship that's been taken over."

"Pirates? I'm one man. Remember that?"

"It's a one-man job. We need somebody who can go in and take them out, one by one."

"I still am not going alone. Someone has to watch my back."

"Do you remember Beau?"

"Hell yeah, I remember Beau. That man could eat crawfish like nobody else I've ever seen," Jax said. "Then again he's huge. He can't hide anywhere. He's too damn big."

"Well, he won't be eating crawfish this time. And he won't need to hide for long. As a matter of fact, he'll be shooting bullets at pirates. He always was a dang good sharpshooter. So he'll meet you there."

"Meet me where?"

Griffin snorted. "Off the Florida coast. You should be there right on time."

"No," Jax said. "I just got off the goddamn plane in California."

"So you're already packed, right? You hear your name on the PA system? Yeah, that's to go pick up your tickets. You're flying out now."

And, with that, Griffin hung up.

Jax swore.

CHAPTER 2

JAX GOT OFF the plane and took several deep breaths, trying to acclimate to the humidity of the Florida air. He shook his head, picked up his duffel bag, and stormed toward the double doors of the airport. As soon as he exited the air-conditioned environment, he had to stop and take several more long, deep breaths. He didn't get a chance to do anything else when a huge bear of a man walked up and gave him a hug. He hugged him back before stepping slightly away. Then he looked up at the man he knew as Beau.

"You're one of the few men who hug me," Jax said.

"More men should do it," Beau said with a big grin. "You ready for this?"

"Hell no," Jax said. "This is all stupid. What the hell will two of us do against pirates who have already seized a cruise ship?"

"Military is ready to send in a crew. We're going in first, that's all."

At that, Jax raised his eyebrows and said, "Well, that's welcome news."

"I know. I thought the same when I heard," Beau said. "Would prefer to see a team of six or eight with us."

"And how are we getting there?"

"Well, I'd like to say that our transport is a fancy chopper to the destroyer so all our tactical gear will be coming with us, but I think we're taking an underwater SEAL delivery vehicle as close as we can, then climb onto the cruise ship quietly. Thank God this is a smaller ship. Can you imagine if we were facing one of the mega ones? Of course it's just us here, and that's bad enough."

Jax rolled his eyes. "Just the two of us …"

"Yes," Beau said. "But, hey, we'll be there as soon as we can."

"Why Florida?"

"We're flying military planes from here on in," Beau said.

"Did you have something to do with the arrangements?"

"No, other than being handed them. My orders were to pick you up and to back you up."

"Well, thanks for coming," Jax said. He ran a hand down his face and said, "I just finished being Griffin's backup."

"I heard," Beau said. "It's almost as if the Mavericks are picking those of us who are ready for a change. One job to try it out and all that."

"And what if that one last job isn't successful?" Jax asked.

"Doesn't bear thinking about," Beau said. "Never has before."

Jax couldn't argue with that. He followed Beau to the SUV, and very quickly they headed to the docks and then onto a military airplane. That started a very long and arduous trip across the ocean until they landed on the destroyer. Almost immediately they set about mapping out their route. "Where the hell is the cruise ship?"

"Off the coast of Panama," Beau said.

"I didn't realize pirates were an issue down there," Jax

said quietly.

"Normally they're not," Beau said. "But apparently they're looking for fresher waters."

"Well, hell, if they just stole the personal belongings off everybody on the cruise ship, that's loads of stuff but not much cash money, I bet. Everything is credit cards and onboard credit and online payments nowadays," Jax said.

"I think they're after a little more than that."

"Do we know what?"

"A female passenger," Beau said.

Jax's heart sank. "That's bad news. Who is she? The daughter of some wealthy mogul somewhere in the world?"

"No, she's not. She's a doctor. Apparently the pirates reached out for the cruise ship's manifest and their passenger list. Her name is there, so they're searching room by room for her."

"Do we know why they want her?"

"She devised some new surgery that one of their doctors utilized, and the patient isn't improving. In fact he's dying."

Jax came to a dead halt, turned, and said, "What?"

Beau shrugged those massive shoulders of his and said, "You know it takes very little to create a war."

"So, she's in a different country, and she creates a new method that works for her but not for a bunch of other doctors? More specifically, for a doctor who's working on some member of a highly valued family, and now she's to fix his mistake?"

"I think they want to take her back to heal this patient."

"In other words, they'll hold her responsible but give her one chance to fix her mistake," Jax said sarcastically.

"Something like that."

"And how do we know this?"

"One of the crew members got the word out. Then social media's buzzing with most of this. Too many passengers to stop word from getting out. Fortunately the pirates are fairly low-tech and don't realize how quickly all this information is traveling around the world now. It's become a very high-profile case," Beau said.

"So you would think that, being an American cruise liner full of Americans, the American government would have sent in a couple teams," Jax said. He still struggled to believe he was heading there with one backup.

"They are. They're coming in behind us. But they want you to find her first."

"Me?" Jax looked at Beau sideways. "What will you do in the meantime?"

"I'll help you find her," he said cheerfully. "Hopefully before the pirates find us."

"Great," Jax said. "The odds suck. Of course that's the way we like it."

"Exactly. I have the ship's blueprints, the passenger list, and some data on the doc; but we do not have any history on the players involved."

"We don't know any of the pirates?"

"No, and neither do we know the family with the sick patient."

"Interesting," he said. He finished tucking his gear into his SEAL delivery vehicle, then turned to have Beau check the air tanks on Jax's back and everything else he carried. Jax reciprocated. When they were given the go-ahead by the seaman on shore, the two of them hopped into their SDV's and were dispatched into the ocean. They blasted out very quickly, and Jax estimated, from the time of launch depending on the speed they should have about a ten- to fifteen-minute swim max, to the base of the cruise liner. Then they'd get on board, strip off their gear, and get to work.

It took twelve minutes. And for that, Jax blamed the currents that surged up from below. They were darn strong and pulled on him every bit of the way. When he finally clambered up to the loading level on the cruise liner and slipped inside—just as the sun rose on a pretty Saturday morning—he took a moment to take stock and to let his breathing return to normal. He quickly stripped off his scuba gear and dry suit, tucked it into a corner of the room in case they needed it, and waited for Beau to do the same. Then, dressed in night-ops attire, they readied themselves, weapons at their ankles. They split up, both with comms in shoulder harnesses to stay in touch with each other.

While Beau went right and would work from the topside down, Jax went left and worked his way to the bottom level where the mechanicals of the ship were. He didn't figure how he'd find the missing woman, but maybe some of the employees on board would be a little more amiable to helping them out. Depends if the pirates had captured the engineer or even the captain. Then the rest of the crew would be rendered uncooperative. Jax pulled out his phone and uploaded the file on the woman, Abigail Eleanor. He frowned at that. Two first names. How did that work?

Each of the ship's main departments had doors with windows inset in them. As Jax neared what should be the engine room, he listened first, then chose his moment to catch a sidelong glance from one edge of the door's window. The engine room had two pirates standing watch, and everybody under guard was male. Jax didn't go in and free the men but sent a message back to his contact at the Mavericks base and to Beau. Then Jax moved on.

A gunshot had him freezing in his tracks. Bastards. Had they shot someone?

He turned around and crept back. Both guards were walking around, laughing and joking. They had their rifles, but both were slung over their shoulders. Not that they couldn't whip them up and shoot anybody quickly, but, as one pirate walked toward the engine room door, coming toward Jax, he realized his decision to let them be had been taken away from him. He needed to deal with this guy now or be seen.

He crouched down low, and, as soon as the door opened, he came up underneath the first guard's rifle, swung it around, and fired one shot, killing the other pirate guard. Then Jax wrapped the rifle's sling around the first man's neck and pulled it tight, snapping his neck. He walked inside, dragging the first pirate, and looked at the four men tied up on the floor. He pulled out his knife, quickly cut them loose, and asked them if they were okay.

All the men nodded. They hopped up, jumped around, and said, "Who are you?"

Jax quickly explained.

"What are we supposed to do now?"

"I want you to stay here," he said. "I'll locate and take down the other pirates, but I can't have you moving around the ship. Do you hear me?"

The men looked completely relieved at the idea.

"I'm counting on you people being here when I come back."

"Not a problem," the first man said. "This is where we belong, no doubt about it. We'll lock ourselves in."

Jax smacked him on the shoulder and said, "Good man. And don't tell anybody else. No communication at all—got it?"

They nodded.

"Even the captain?" one asked.

Jax shook his head. "This is the first level of the ship that I've searched so far. I don't know what pressure the captain is under already. We can't let him have this info."

The men look confused, and Jax said, "What if the captain's wife is on board, and the pirates are holding a gun to her head? If the captain tells the pirates that I've just released you guys, they'll come after you and me, and they'll take her out at the same time. Probably taking out the captain too, after he sees his wife die."

The men all nodded. "So communication silence until we're out of this."

"At least you're ahead of the game. You're free and clear right now. Please stay locked up."

And, with that, Jax quickly disappeared. The door closed and locked behind him. Good. But his priority was finding this Abigail person. Even the name stuck in his throat. Mentally he shortened it to Abby. Now, if only she was healthy and capable of doing some of the things he needed her to do. He had no clue about her age, but he suspected she would likely be sixty years old plus gray-haired, yet hopefully fit since she was a doctor. Otherwise he would have a heck of a time getting her off this ship. And he had no doubt he needed to do that and fast.

With the bottom level cleared, he moved upward. He went room by room by room. He took out two more pirate gunmen, confiscating their weapons and leaving everybody else in place. By the time he came up to the stateroom levels, he knew his search would take longer. He had texted Beau to come meet him here, down on the far side, checking the same level as Jax was but from the opposite end of the ship. They checked for anybody in hiding. He met many people who were still hiding away in their rooms, thinking that they could stay there. And he agreed with that, but nobody seemed to know anything about Abigail Eleanor.

Then he and Beau repeated their search on the other stateroom levels, working their way upward.

By the time Jax was done with this stateroom level, he was frustrated and aggravated. He came up another level to the kitchens. At least one set of kitchens. And found two more pirate guards. He swore as he saw them because these guards weren't joking, talking, or doing anything except holding their rifles on a bunch of people while the pirates sampled the food set off to the side. And the look on their faces said they'd just as soon kill every one of them. He had no way to know if Abigail was in there. He quickly tapped out a message to Beau, letting him know the status on the kitchen.

His response came back. **Coming up on your six.**

Jax waited until he heard the tap on his comm unit, indicating Beau was in reach. With him on the far side, the two of them opened the double doors to the kitchen. Jax dove to the floor, reached up, and fired a single shot as one pirate gunman leveled his rifle in Jax's direction. Jax put a bullet in his forehead and dropped him. Screams came from all around him, and he quickly swung his weapon to check that Beau's man was down.

"Stop," he said, holding up one finger. "We need silence. We can't let the rest of the pirates know that you guys are free."

In an instant, the screams muted to sobs as they hugged and held each other carefully.

"You've got enough knives in here, so untie yourselves and confirm that each of you are unharmed," he said. "But not one of you is allowed to leave this room until we tell you to. Do you hear me? You're putting everybody else in danger if you so much as step foot from this room."

Until he extracted a promise from every one of them, and he wasn't even sure then, he stepped back slightly, looked at the two chefs, and said, "You're both in charge. I hate to say it, but, if anyone of them moves out of here, you're to stop them. If that means kill them, that means kill them."

More gasps were heard, but he shook his head and said, "No, we're not playing here. You'll end up getting more people killed if you leave here. And I don't care if you've got brothers, siblings, lovers, or children outside. You stay in here, or it'll be open gunfire soon. And we can't have more people letting the pirates know that we're already on board."

The two chefs immediately stationed themselves at the doors, weapons in hand.

On that note, Jax and Beau left.

HOW THE HELL did she get into these situations? Abigail had no idea what she was supposed to do right now. When word came that the place was overrun with pirates, she immediately went looking for a good hiding place. *The ductwork.* Staying up here was temporary though. She couldn't stay here forever. How long before somebody decided that it was better to sink the cruise ship? Or to blast gunfire all through the place, and she'd die that way by taking a bullet? She wasn't even sure what strange reason made her hop up into the ductwork and hide when everybody else was rushing through the hallways.

She'd been here for at least an hour, still thinking of what to do. She'd heard some noises outside. Apparently the pirates were looking for her. And that just blew her away, not to mention terrified her. Now she couldn't trust anyone because she didn't know who would turn her over to the pirates. She didn't even know how many pirates were here and what weaponry they had. All she knew is that they wanted her for some reason. She groaned when she thought about it. It had to be connected to her work. That's all the world knew her for. Why else would anyone come for her? Her techniques were already controversial in the traditional medical world but gaining traction with each success.

Yet her techniques worked, more often than not. But then she knew what she was doing. A lot of doctors had joined the bandwagon and claimed that their methodologies and their protocols had enabled her to jump to the front of the research game.

She understood that because research was all about being the first person who could show results. And unfortunately too often, the results that the researchers showed weren't any good. So the main goal was always to keep people funding your research. Universities would let doctors go if they weren't bringing in enough grant money. Her claim to fame was a stem-cell collection system, and so much research was going on everywhere with many new systems arriving almost daily. Stem cells were big money. Her system was fast, simple, and reliable. So she didn't understand why anybody would have any problem with it, but apparently people did. Or, at least, they weren't seeing the same results.

She didn't understand that either, and she really didn't

understand why these pirates would give a damn. They wouldn't. So why the hell were they after her?

Just then she heard sounds in the room beneath her.

She closed her eyes and prayed.

CHAPTER 3

When whoever it was walked out of the room, Abigail took a slow breath and gently released it. She could only hope that having checked this room to find it empty, nobody would come back in again. She breathed a heavy sigh of relief this time, grateful that the only reason the ductwork sustained her up here was because of her petite size. She scooted along, thinking about exactly where in the ship she was. The ductwork seemed to run all along the place, but the last thing she wanted to do was get caught up in some heavy-duty equipment that would kill her faster than anything.

She moved as quietly as she could. She'd long given up on her shoes, leaving them back in her room under the bed. And now, with her bare toes pushing her forward on her belly, she scooched another twenty feet forward. She came up against a branching of the ductwork. A noise distracted her, only she didn't recognize what she heard. Some engine or motor purred to her left. The last thing she wanted to do was go toward that.

She shifted to the right and headed down what she hoped would be the center of the ship. She didn't even want to come on this damn cruise in the first place, but her mother and her sister had insisted that Abigail needed a break and that she should take one of these cruises to get her completely away from her job. She'd finally given in and booked it on her own, secretly looking forward to some time alone.

They didn't understand that she had brought her work with her and that her job was exactly what she lived for. She'd met lots of friends over the years, and several had tried to stay but somehow her work had dominated and they'd drifted away. She'd had relationships but nothing that went the distance. None appealed. At least not in the way they wanted to appeal. Not in any way.

She didn't know how she was supposed to overcome this distrust of relationships. It's not that hers had been bad. They'd been good. They'd been loving. But they'd all ended up with this boredness to them. She figured they just had to address it before they got too far down that pathway. In several cases though, the men had found other women to add excitement to their lives.

She kept moving ahead until she heard another odd sound. Was that gunfire? Her blood froze, and her body stiffened in shock.

Up until now, she hadn't considered people were dying. She'd heard the screams and the shouts but nothing else. But gunfire now definitely changed that. She shifted off to the side and looked through an access panel but found an empty room below. So where the hell was she? Between the eighth and ninth decks? Or did she get as high as the seventh? It didn't really matter though, except that it determined how hard it would be to get topside if the pirates sank the ship.

She definitely wanted to go up if she could, as in higher up. Above the pilot's station would be nice. At least then she'd have some hope of surviving a sinking ship. She crept forward, looking for signs of life at each grate she came across, but she found nothing. At the next grate, she saw a hallway and elevators. One was open and sitting, waiting. A stairwell should be nearby, for those who didn't want to take the elevator, but she couldn't see if from this grate.

What would happen if she went that way in this ductwork?

She headed in that direction, but it didn't lead her to the elevator shaft. And she wasn't sure how to go from the ductwork she was in up to the next level. However, her ductwork branched off again now, connected to at least ten to twenty feet of pipes, but they were all smooth sided. Up, down, left, right, crisscrossed. She wasn't sure how to get out of this maze or where she was or how to move upward.

She wondered at the options facing her, then headed back to where the stairs and the elevators were, and slipped out of an access panel in the ductwork into one of the closest rooms. Then she stepped into the stairwell and quietly raced upward again. As she opened the stairwell door at the top, she heard a voice beside her. She turned to see a man dressed completely in black, his face covered with black markings. ... He was armed. She stared at him, completely frozen.

He nudged her gently with his hand. "What's your name?"

The last thing she would give would be her name. In spite of her best efforts, her nickname slipped out.

"Abby," she said. "I'm Abby."

JAX STARED AT Abby. "As in Abigail Eleanor?"

She nodded slowly, but the look on her face was one of terror.

He grabbed her before she had a chance to run, his fingers wrapping snugly around her upper arm. He pulled her close against him. "Well, I'm Jax, from the US government," he said. "Apparently the pirates are looking for you. Do you know why?"

She stared at him in disbelief.

"Answer me," he said. "Do you know why?"

Finally she shook her head.

"Social media says your methods don't work. They need you to help somebody in their family."

"So it *is* connected to my work," she said in a daze.

"Only because their doctor botched it," he whispered.

She shook her head. "That makes no sense. I have pioneered a way of collecting stem cells. Lots of doctors are doing it around the world now. It's not something you can really botch."

"Well, maybe it's more a case of," he said, "it didn't work."

"Meaning, it didn't make the person well?" she said with a shrug. "Of course not. It's only one technique in a long line of medical arsenals."

"Right," he said. "Well, apparently the pirates want to kidnap you and take you back to wherever this family member is, so you can fix him."

She stared at him. "But I don't even know what the problem is."

"Well, I don't think they're too interested in waiting around and asking questions," he said gently.

She nodded slowly. "So you'll turn me in then?"

"No," he said, frowning. "Why would I do that? I'll take you back to one of our ships and then come in and take out the rest of the pirates."

He saw the relief on her face, but then she frowned. "What about all the other people here?"

"What about them?" he asked.

"I can't have them hurt because of me."

"Understood," he said. And then he smiled. "But what will you do about it?"

"I don't know," she said. "I've been hiding in the ductwork, figuring out exactly what to do. I was thinking that, if the pirates sink the ship, I should at least make my way up a few more decks, but I was trying to avoid contact with anybody."

"Well, guess what?" he asked. "You screwed that up." But he let humor rest in his voice. He studied her; she couldn't be more than five foot tall. She looked like she was eighteen. He hardly believed that she was even a doctor. Suspicious all of a sudden, he asked, "Do you have any ID on you?"

Her eyebrows shot up. "No, I wasn't trying to save anything but me when I heard that pirates were taking over the ship."

"Surprisingly,"—he stepped back—"it's the first thing every woman normally does. They grab their purses."

"Maybe, but I'm not *every* woman," she said coolly.

Just then a noise came from the left. He pulled her beside him, up against the door, and held his fingers to his lips.

She rolled her eyes at him. "Like I don't know to stay quiet."

He tilted his head at her but didn't say anything. Jax waited and waited and waited, but no more of the same noise came. He frowned at that. He wanted to poke his head through to the other side but knew it was almost a guarantee of getting his head shot off. He studied his options and then said, "We need to change levels."

"Better to go down a level," she whispered. "It was deserted."

"Well, that works in some cases," he said, "but it won't get the rest of the people off this ship."

"I thought you only wanted me off," she said.

He looked at her, smiled, and said, "Good point. Let's go."

And he led her back into the stairway, forcing her down the stairs again and again.

She protested the whole way. "Don't take me off the ship. We must do something to save everybody else."

"I hear you, but I can't take the chance."

"It's me the pirates want. You're not making any sense. If they kill the others to get to me, that's just a numbers game, and obviously we'll all lose that one."

A loud voice snapped orders close by.

CHAPTER 4

ABBY DARTED FROM Jax's arms, racing down the stairs to get away from the voices.

He spouted an expletive as he jumped down the stairs three at a time behind her. Just as they disappeared into the next level below, he heard sounds of the doors above opening. He grabbed her arm, pulled her against an outside wall, and asked, "What are you doing?"

Gasping in panic, she spun, looked at him, and said, "Trying to get away. What does it look like?"

He could feel the tremors in her body and could see her terror in her expression. He held her close and whispered, "Somebody's coming. Be quiet. If it's a pirate, I want to take him out."

She stared up at him, suddenly in shock. Then she nodded. "Do we know how many there are?"

He shrugged. "Six less than when I first came on the ship." Her jaw dropped. She went to speak, but he held a finger against her lips and said, "No more nonsense. Stop. Stay here. Wait." And he placed her behind him around the corner, and then he crept up to the doorway.

The double doors opened wide, and two men walked through. Both held weapons, semiautomatic machine guns.

Jax didn't understand their language but heard something about the engine room and realized that some of the men had tried to call up the pirates who Jax had taken down. There was no time to lose. These pirates couldn't be allowed to reach the engine room and to find out the damage to their numbers already.

Without even thinking, Jax pulled out a handgun and shot the first one dead. As the second one spun, swearing and lifting his rifle, Jax knocked it out of range and plowed his fist hard into the pirate's jaw. But the man didn't go down easy. Instead, he snapped back with his own fists, trying to pull a handgun from his belt holster. Jax was on him, pounding him hard, until the pirate went down. And, with one final kick, Jax shoved the toe of his boot hard into the pirate's jaw. There was a mighty *crack*; something snapped, and the man dropped.

Standing on his feet, gasping hard and his chest heaving, Jax wiped the sweat off his face to see Abby staring at him in absolute horror.

"I've never seen anything like that," she said when she could. She didn't want to replay the actions that she'd just seen, but it was hard not to. She raced to him, her hands out. "Are you hurt?"

He still looked at her, frowned, and then shook his head. "I'll be okay."

"But you killed both of them," she said, "with your bare hands."

"I shot the first one," he said bluntly. "And you were horrified when you saw what I did to the second one, but I had to do it."

"Sure," she said. "I was shocked at first. But it doesn't take very long for the initial shock to become relief when you realize what the pirates would have done to me if they had caught me."

He nodded. "Now let's get these men out of sight." He dragged them out of view, quickly stripped them of all their weapons, and he needed a place to hide them. He checked the staterooms, and it took a while to find ones that he could get into. With that, he quickly dragged in the first man and dumped him in the closet. The second one, he put in the bathroom and then shut and locked the door behind him. Armed with their weapons, he turned to find her with one over her shoulder and a handgun tucked into her belt and another one in her hand. He looked at her and froze.

She lowered the handgun, smiled, and said, "I'm not one of the bad guys."

"Good thing," he said, "because I'd break your jaw too."

She winced. "That was meant as a jest," she said quietly. "And, of course, you're right. There's nothing funny about this."

"But humor does make it easier to deal with," he said. He picked up the other weapons and quickly placed them on his person. "I still want you down and off this ship."

"No," she said, more certain of what she needed to do. Even though the idea terrified her. But, with Jax here, he might be enough to change the balance of this numbers game. She shook her head. "I don't want everybody here to pay the price for the pirates not finding me."

"So what do you want me to do?" he asked, his voice harsh. "Use you as a bargaining chip?"

She gave him a one-arm shrug and nodded. "Obviously you can take care of yourself," she said with a motion toward the room where he'd stashed the dead man. "And that changes things."

"It changes nothing," he said. "Absolutely nothing." Just then he stopped and tilted his head, as if listening to something.

Nervous, she glanced around and said, "What? Is somebody coming?"

He flashed a bright smile, an oddly charming look, considering the blood still on his face. "Yeah. Somebody is. We'll wait here."

"Somebody on your team or on the bad guys' team?" she asked, insistent for information. She hated to be caught unaware again. It had been such a shock, and her adrenaline still rushed through her. She knew that, as soon as it slowed down, she would crash, and she couldn't afford for that to happen.

"Do you have your phone with you?"

She nodded.

"Let me key in my number."

She frowned, didn't move.

"In case we get separated."

Only then she forked over her phone, which he returned to her soon thereafter.

"I added Beau's too. He's my partner."

She whispered, "How can you live like this all the time?"

"Well, when you're used to it, the adrenaline is there more to help you stay in control because you learn to harness that. For someone like you, this is new and shocking, so the adrenaline is a fight-or-flight instinct. It's not the same thing for me."

"Can't be good for your heart," she announced.

"Well, it's not like most of us live very long anyway," he said, his tone cryptic.

She stopped, stared at him, in shock once again. "Oh, my gosh. I guess that's right, isn't it?"

He nodded. "It is right. It's one of the reasons I decided

I was done with my old life."

His words and his tone made her curious. "So you're not doing this anymore?"

"No, it's got nothing to do with this job."

"Except for the fact that it's really important that you survive it," she said softly. "If you've done this work before, and you've saved other people, then you need your day in the sun. You need a chance to rest."

"Resting is often a euphemism for boredom," he said. "I don't have future plans yet, but I don't plan on being bored."

"Sounds good to me. I doubt I'll ever quit working. I'll always have something research-wise going on."

"Well, that's not necessarily a bad thing."

"You obviously like weapons," she said, watching as he shifted the handgun from hand to hand.

"I do," he said. "I always figured I could design something better."

"Well, there's a hobby for you."

He nodded. "I've been working on it at home in my spare time, but jobs like this don't really give you much spare time."

She snorted. "We'd make a great pair. You'd be creating machines that kill, and I'd be creating systems that save."

"Hey, that's the way the world works," he said. "And that makes us two halves of the whole." Even at that, he snorted.

"Hey, it's not that funny," she said. "I'm sure you're probably not as much of a loner as I am. But I'd like to think, at some point in time, there's a partner out there for me, in the relationship sense."

He shot her a sideways look.

She shrugged. "What did I say?"

"Well, I'm definitely a loner," he said. "Hard to be involved in anything but my work. But odd to bring up relationship-type partners here."

"All partnerships are relationships too. But I guess I was thinking more about my lack of a relationship." She gave him a bright smile. "Sorry. Just a little bleed through there."

"I'm hardly a good candidate for a relationship—just so we're clear. I'm gone a lot and often in very dangerous scenarios."

She thought about that and then nodded. "I guess it would be hard to watch you leave and do things like this all the time. But it depends on the woman and where her passion lies." She glanced around and said, "So, where's this person we're meeting?"

Just then the doors opened. She let out a small shriek and jumped closer to Jax. He grinned and said, "Abby, meet Beau. Beau, meet Abby."

In walked one of the biggest men she had ever seen.

His eyes were glacial hard, until his gaze landed on her. He smiled, shook his head, and said, "I thought you were a doctor. You don't look like you should be out of high school."

She snorted and said, "I'm Dr. Abigail Eleanor, and I'm almost thirty years old." She reached out her hand and, in a more formal voice, said, "I'm pleased to meet you."

He took her hand gently in his, almost engulfing her small hand. "Well, thirty's never looked so good," he said.

Beau's lips tilted, but his gaze was already fixed on Jax.

"If you like children, you mean," she said with a grin.

"Are you ready to go?"

Jax nodded. "I've got seven down. You?"

"Damn," Beau said. "I'm only five down. I left one alive."

"Well, I think one was still alive, but he won't be for long," Jax said.

"Exactly," Beau said. "Now that we got her, we need to get her off."

"One problem with that," Jax said.

"What's that?" Beau's gaze went from one to the other.

Abby spoke up. "I don't want to leave and be safe and have all these people here in danger, possibly killed or injured because the pirates can't find me."

Beau leaned back on his heels, rocked a few times, and said, "Well, I don't really see any way around that."

Her eyebrows shot up. "Surely you can do something. Use me as a bargaining chip or something to get all these people off the ship."

"Too many people. Nobody's able to pick them up."

"I guess that's the problem with cruise ships. Megaships, megapeople." She frowned, not having thought about that. "Well, how about all the pirates leave with me?"

"That's not a good idea either," Beau said. He stepped back, then tapped the comm on his ear several times. She watched as he had a conversation with something that wasn't even there. He looked at Jax. "Orders are to take her off the ship. Unless you've got another idea?"

She stared at Jax hopefully.

"I can see her point," he said gently. "The pirates need to know that she's not here, if that's the case though. We can't have anybody else being punished."

Just then sounds crackled in their intercom. Beau turned a little bit away and swore. He then faced Jax and said, "They're shooting passengers."

"That's it," she said, and she bolted for the double doors. Only she didn't get far. Beau grabbed one arm, and Jax grabbed the other, pulling her back. She almost got slingshotted back into their arms. She struggled hard. "You can't let them kill other people because of me. It's one life versus twenty-five hundred. That's not fair."

"And what would you like to do?" Jax asked.

"Let me go to them. Let them take me. If you want, come with me. You can be my boyfriend or my brother or something," she snapped. "And you can protect me while we find a way to get away then. But not at the cost of the deaths of the other passengers."

Jax stilled. He glanced at Beau. Beau's eyebrows shot up as he studied the two of them. "Don't do it," he said. "It's suicide."

"But she's right," Jax said. "Twenty-five hundred lives for one."

Beau nodded. "I know it sucks, but orders are orders."

Jax snorted. "No, we have no orders in this case. Remember? We're on our own. We do what we do because we're the ones who do it best." He nodded to her and said, "But, other than our names, we're married. Got it? We're not to be separated. You make no side deals. I'll escort you up and tell them who we are."

"But your name won't be on the manifest."

"Did you come with anybody?"

"No, I was supposed to. Benny was to come with me," she said.

"And who's that?"

"My cousin."

"Last name?"

Her eyebrows slowly rose as she nodded. "Eleanor. Benny Eleanor."

"Could be a guy," Beau said.

"Exactly."

"But if they check you for ID and find you have something else?"

He gave her a wolfish smile. "They won't find anything." He looked at Beau and said, "Track us."

Beau immediately dug into the bag that he carried and pulled out two syringes. He quickly set them up, and, exposing Jax's arm, he slammed the plunger home. He set the second one and turned to her. "Pull out your arm, Doc."

"What is that?" she asked nervously. But it was too late. The sting already happened. She swore and looked down at the slightly reddened area. "What did you just do?"

"Put homing devices in both of you so I can track you. I won't be far behind."

And this became way too real. She stared down at her arm, then at Jax. "Dear God, this is really shitty. But there's nothing else we can do though, is there?"

"YES, THERE IS," Jax said calmly. "I can take you off. The pirates could search the ship, and they won't find you."

"They'll blame everybody else then, won't they?"

"It's possible," he said. "They already are."

"Fine," she said. "Let's go. But we can hardly go up fully armed."

He nodded, slowly handed off as many of his weapons to Beau as he could. Fully divested of everything extra, Jax turned toward Beau and said, "I need to switch out of these clothes."

"Right," Beau said. "You don't look very holidayish."

They quickly found a stateroom where a man had been staying. Jax rummaged around and found a T-shirt that was a little too tight for comfort, but, hey, it would do. With his clothes changed to looking like he was a civilian on vacation, he grabbed her arm and said, "I still think this is a shitty idea."

And obviously, she'd had a moment to think about it because she nodded and said, "So do I."

He froze, turned to look at her, and said, "You've got one chance to change your mind, and we can get you safely out to the military ships surrounding the area."

"No," she said. "I won't have any more of these deaths on my conscience. I might die doing this, but I do what I think is right."

He admired that, but it was still foolish. He looked at Beau, who shrugged and said, "Your call. She's pretty easy to carry. We can knock her out and take her with us, put an oxygen mask on her, and drag her all the way back to the ships."

Oxygen mask? At that, she panicked.

Jax sighed, closed his eyes, thought about it, and then nodded. "Twenty-five hundred to one," he said slowly. "Tell the others that I'll see them on the other side."

CHAPTER 5

ABBY WASN'T SURE what he meant by that *see you on the other side* reference, but it seemed so final. And she realized that what she had decided to do also put his life in danger. "No," she said. "You stay here."

"You don't get to call those shots," Jax said. "You're the one who's refusing to obey orders."

"So are you," she said.

He gripped her arm tightly and said, "Sure I am, but I'm allowed to."

"Well, your orders don't apply to me," she said.

"Maybe," he said. "We'll see how you feel when you've been in captivity for a long time. And remember. Just because I'm with you doesn't mean I'll be allowed to leave the ship with you. It doesn't mean that I'll be allowed to go with you in any way, shape, or form. And it doesn't mean I can protect you, even if the pirates say that you'll be safe."

She could feel the chills running through her soul, realizing what a gamble she had taken. At the same time, how could she not? Everyone else aboard this ship could die if she didn't show up. She took a deep breath, squeezed her fingers tight, and said, "It's either die trying to do what's right or die a little every day knowing what I did was cowardly and wrong."

He looked at her for a long moment, then nodded.

"Let's go." And he gripped her hand in his. "And don't let go of me."

She nodded, and he snagged a jacket from the same closet and said, "This might cover one of the weapons," as he put a handgun in his back pocket. And, on that note, he nodded to Beau.

She hated to see the concern in the other man's eyes, knowing this could be a death trip but still making the choice to do it anyway.

"Let the others know," Jax said.

"Will do," Beau said, and then he swore long and loud. It didn't matter because Jax was already in hell.

She stared at Beau and said, "I don't want you to die too. Please do what you can to save us but save yourself first."

He glared at her. "That goes against what all of us always do," he said. "No one will like this decision."

She smiled, nodded, opened up the double doors, and headed through. As soon as they were on their own, she asked Jax, "What's the best way?"

"I suggest we get ourselves captured," he said. "Let somebody lead us to the pirates. If we walk into a crowd of them, it's hard to say what their reaction will be."

"You have your communication device. So you'll tell your people how many pirates we see and anything else that might help, so that we get out of this alive?"

"Don't worry. I'll be tracking and giving my unit a running commentary as much as I can," he said. "What I can't do is blow Beau's cover."

She pondered that, trying to figure out what he meant.

And then he clarified. "If they find my comm unit, we're out of luck, and I'll be separated and potentially killed right off the bat."

She sucked in her breath, realizing now what was involved, and nodded. "So we'll give Beau exactly what we can and hope for the best."

"Exactly," he murmured.

They moved toward the upper levels. As they walked along one of the decks, there was a shout, and then a man ran toward Jax. The pirate held a rifle on them, snapping orders constantly in Jax's face. Finally he switched to English. "Who are you?"

"I'm Dr. Abigail Eleanor," she said. "And Mr. Benny Eleanor, my husband." She was proud of the fact that she didn't even trip over the name. She looked at the pirate. "I believe you guys are looking for us." The gunman's face lit with joy, and he quickly spoke into his handset. She listened but didn't understand the language at all. They were quickly shepherded to the upper deck, where they were led to a group of men standing off to one side.

As they walked closer, she could tell Jax was sending information, but his lips never moved. She didn't get it, but whatever he did seemed to be working. And just before they were quickly grabbed and searched, she realized that the headpiece around his ear was no longer there. She cried out as he was pulled off to one side. He reached out a hand. She grabbed it and yelled, "Stop."

The pirates froze. The leader stepped forward and said, "You are not to tell us to stop."

"Maybe not," she said, "but, if you want my assistance, you *will* stop. And you will leave my husband alone."

The man studied her face for a long moment; then he looked at the others and nodded. They let Jax go.

Jax immediately stepped out, wrapped an arm around

her, and tucked her up close. "What is going on?" he asked.

"What's going on," the gunman said, "is the doctor's services are needed."

⚓

THEY WERE THRUST into the center of the group of pirates again and shepherded off to one side. Instructions were sent back and forth. But Jax could feel a sense of unrest between the pirates. The men were happy to have found what they came for, but they wanted more out of this. Did they know how badly reduced their team's numbers were? Jax had already sent the count on the number of pirates here to Beau. Eight men surrounded them, plus the one man who had brought them up.

Jax could have taken him out at any time, and it really chafed not being able to. If he had a chance to take them out right now, he would. But him against them wasn't great odds, especially with Abby right beside him. She could be taken down by stray bullets. He had been pretty damn sure that Beau still picked off the other pirates on this ship. It was the best avenue for them all.

If Jax could cut down some of these pirates, without putting Abigail in danger, he would. And then Abby wouldn't have to go anywhere with the pirates, and Jax and Beau could take her to their ship. Then the pirates here split off, some going left, some going right, but four stayed with him and Abby. Well, that was helpful because four men gave a whole lot better odds to Jax than nine.

She bit her lip as she glanced around at four dead passengers with bullets through their chests, all heaped on one side. She stopped, her chest constricting. As she looked at the pirates, one of the four gunmen shoved her and said, "We were looking for you, and they wouldn't talk."

"Of course they wouldn't," she said softly. "They don't know who I am. Why would they?"

He shrugged. "Doesn't matter. They don't know anybody now."

Jax tugged her closer into his arms, seeing the tears in her eyes. Nothing was easy about terrorist actions. They killed wantonly as long as it furthered their cause. Everybody was collateral damage. But it sent shock waves through his soul to realize just how much he wanted to protect her from anything ugly again. She didn't deserve this. But then the four dead tourists didn't deserve an early death either.

Just then two pirates from his group were sent off, in a different direction. The remaining two men motioned Jax toward a hallway. He opened the door, shoved her through first, and then, now alone with the two pirates following him, Jax turned, pulling the handgun hidden at the back of his waistband and fired two shots, taking out both men. He quickly opened the closest door and found a large bathroom. He dragged both men inside, chucking their weapons. Now fully armed again, he raced back to her side, and they kept on walking.

She stared at him. "What did you do?" she cried out. "How will this help our cause?"

"There were nine," he said calmly. "Now we're down to seven. Beau just took out three more as well."

"So, he evened the odds," she said. Then she shook her head. "Is this a game to you?"

"It's not a game," he said, "but do you need that pile of dead passengers to remember just what this is?"

Another door was up ahead. Acting casual, he opened

the door and moved her inside a women's washroom. He looked around, nodded, and said, "Nice. I want you to stay here for a moment."

"For how long?"

He held the door open a sliver. "Until the next two pirates come down," he said. "We don't know how many are left in total. I suspected at least twenty to begin with, but we've cut their numbers in half. If Beau and I can keep cutting them down, we won't worry about anybody being taken off the ship."

Hope lit up her eyes. She nodded slowly. "If you think you can …"

He grinned, leaned forward, and kissed her hard before pulling back. "Sweetie, I know I can. Now be a good wife and stay here."

He slipped out the door, closing it slightly, and, with a last brief glance in her direction, disappeared down the hallway. And caught sight of the two pirates he was looking for. But he needed to take them out as fast as he had taken anybody out so far. And definitely before any messages were sent between them.

He had a maneuver he'd learned in his martial arts class, but it was hard to do on two people at the same time. Jax took several running steps and made a flying jump, his hands out, both at specific angles. He needed to grab both men at the back of their necks and hit their pressure points.

Jax landed hard. They cried out, twisting and falling, but he maintained his grip as they went down and then quickly let go of his left hand, which had the worst of the grips, and thrust his knee into that man's jaw and followed it through with a quick half step from his left foot into the man's throat. The pirate never made a sound.

The other one was trying to aim his rifle in Jax's face but struggled against the grip Jax held locked on his neck. It was hard for anybody to move if Jax caught the right pressure point. Slowly the man sagged to his knees and then fell face-first into the hallway. Jax quickly released his hands, shaking them out before they cramped up, and assessed the damage. Now he had to get rid of these men and fast. He quickly separated their weapons and comm devices from the men and headed toward the first doorway.

Most of these doors were locked, but there was a simple and easy way to get past that. He pulled out his tools and quickly unlocked the room, stepped inside to make sure it was completely empty, and then dragged both men in. There, he found bedding and tied them up. Only as he tied the second one did he note this pirate was dead.

The first pirate was still alive, though unconscious, and he couldn't be allowed to get loose. Jax quickly knotted him up around the feet and then around the hands—behind his back—and promptly tied them both together. He gagged the pirate's mouth too, stopping him from making a sound when he did wake up. And Jax added a special noose around the man's neck and tied it to the ties he had behind the pirate. This way, if he struggled too much, it would tighten the noose around his neck.

Having done what he could, Jax replenished his own weapons, taking two small handguns and several knives off these pirates. Then he stepped out and raced toward the women's washroom.

As he stepped in, the door slammed hard against his face. When he had a chance to recover, he saw a handgun pointed at his head. His jaw locked as he stared into the eyes of a man with murder in his gaze.

Heavily armed, the pirate sent an icy smile in Jax's direction. "Think you're so smart, do you?" he growled. "I don't know if you're responsible for some of our men disappearing, but we'll make sure you're not around to do anything more." And then he pulled his finger back on the trigger as if to shoot Jax in the face.

Out of nowhere the pirate's head was slammed into the door. Abby slowly lowered her leg from the high kick she'd delivered to his temple, even as Jax pushed the gun from his face, followed up with a right uppercut thrust into the pirate's jaw, shoving it back and up. The man's head snapped again. The only sound was the *thud* as he hit the floor. Jax quickly stepped in and closed the bathroom door. He looked at Abby and said, "Are you okay?"

She shook so badly that he pulled her into his arms just to hold her close. She mumbled something against his chest. He stepped back so he could look down at her. "What was that?"

"You're suffocating me," she said on a breathless note. "I'm fine. He wasn't here very long. He stepped in, took one look at me, and then heard you coming down the hallway."

"Shit," he said. "I was trying to be quiet, but I wasn't thinking about that as much as getting back to get you. I took out the other two men, and I've got them both in another room, but I wasn't thinking anybody else had time to come in here. That was my fault."

"I don't really care whose fault it is," she said, wrapping her arms around her chest. She glanced up at him and then down. "Are you okay? Did he hurt you?"

Jax smiled. "No, I'm fine. Nobody's hurt me."

"Good," she said with relief. "How many more men can they have? And is this one still alive?"

He looked at her, smiled, and said, "You haven't bothered checking. Are you worried?"

She shook her head. "No," she said. "I refuse to help mend an injury I intended to cause."

He laughed at that, bent down, and said, "No point in helping this one. He's dead."

"Did you break his neck?"

He studied the pirate's profile and said, "Looks like his nose was crushed into his brain."

She gasped and then crouched beside him. "You know what? I think you're right. Not to mention the man's neck is broken, and his jaw's misaligned."

He nodded. "If you strike out, make sure you do it with purpose." He rose, picked up the gunman, and dragged him to the farthest stall. There, he sat him on the toilet and quickly divested him of all his weapons. "Now we're gathering a huge armory, and I have no place to keep it all," he complained good-naturedly.

She quickly brought him a garbage can from under the counter. "Well, you can put a bunch of it in here. We can always come back for it later, if we need it."

He looked at her in surprise and then nodded. "I should have asked you before, but I suppose you know how to shoot a gun, right?"

She laughed. "I'm from Texas."

He held up what the gunman had been carrying and asked, "What would you like?"

She took both handguns and then grabbed one of the rifles. "If you're not turning me over to them," she said, "which I presume from this complete change of plans since we left your buddy, then I'll take as much as I can carry."

He nodded. "Only if you know how to use it."

She checked the semiautomatic and said, "Well, I haven't ever used anything like this before but wow."

"Exactly," he said. "The problem is, you won't have any trouble once you start firing, but it's got more kickback than you're probably used to, and it's harder to control the direction of your aim." He helped her adjust one around her back, and then he pulled out a knife sheath from the gunman and said, "So far I've taken at least a dozen of these away."

She looked at it, surprised, and said, "This one I'll take because it's got a sheath." She bent down, tucked it under her jeans, and into her sock. She held out her leg and asked, "Does it show?"

He shook his head. "Not enough that anybody will notice. If you get searched, they'll find it all anyway." He looked at her, glanced at the closed stall, and said, "Come on. Let's go."

She chuckled and said, "What's your hurry? Haven't you killed enough men yet?"

"Well, that's two more kills and one more injured," he said. "I need to meet up with Beau too."

She nodded seriously. "The last thing we want is for him to get in over his head."

Jax smiled and nodded. "He's got some serious skills. Though the problem is with his size. Often men go for him almost in a mano a mano fight."

"That must be hard for him," she said slowly. "He's not just big, he's oversize."

Jax chuckled. "That's one way to look at it. I'm pretty sure he's pretty happy as he is."

"I think the big guys always are," she said with a smile.

Jax opened the door, holding up his hand to hold her back, and whispered, "Let me check first."

And he disappeared.

CHAPTER 6

ABBY WATCHED JAX leave and waited, hating how she didn't even want the door to close. But his face reappeared suddenly and almost shockingly. She put a hand to her chest and glared at him. "Don't do that," she gasped. "You scared me."

He held out his hand. "Come on."

She put her hand in his without hesitation. Something about a bonding experience like this either made you trust someone or not. But she already knew what Jax was like inside. He'd pretended—or had started off trying to do what she wanted to do—thinking maybe it was one avenue, but all the time his mind was working on solutions.

When the opportunity presented itself to go in a better direction here, he was right there all over it. He proved that time and time again. The fact that he was gorgeous, lean, and mean appealed in ways that she'd never expected. She wasn't usually into alpha males. Normally she went more for the academics. But then they didn't make her blood boil like this one did, whether it was with temper or something else that she wasn't prepared to examine. No doubt Jax caught her attention on every level. There was just something about him. The power, the self-control, and that can-do attitude were all so very sexy.

She had spent most of her life with books and patients

and labs and men so very opposite to Jax.

In the past, she'd always assumed men like him weren't for her. But right now, she was sure thinking that a taste of this alpha male might be exactly what her body needed. Then again, maybe not as he dragged her down the hallway.

At the set of stairs, they stopped. Of course, on this cruise, no doorways were closed off to the stairs. The elevators here could end up trapped, so stairways had to be accessible at all times. He looked at her and said, "Industrial stairs are off to the side for the staff, and I'll try to reach the service elevator."

"Well, there's no *you* at all in this," she snapped. "Where you go, I go."

When he turned and gave her a dangerous look, she just smiled innocently and said, "Remember what happened when you left me alone the last time?"

His gaze narrowed.

She gave him a winning smile and said, "You know I'm safer with you than left behind."

He seemed to think about it for a moment and then gave a quick nod. "But you stay right behind me and stay quiet."

She thought both of those orders were completely unnecessary, but, at the same time, he needed to understand that she was prepared to follow the rules. She kept right on his heels until they got to the service elevator. He pushed the buttons, checked out the inside, stepped in, looked around, shook his head, stepped out again, and then went to a set of double doors off to the side. He opened the double doors and dragged her with him.

Just then one of the handsets he had taken away from the pirates crackled. A man spoke a language Jax didn't understand. He snatched it from his pocket, but, instead of answering, he played with the dials until it became really staticky. And then he shut it off.

She looked at it, frowned, and said, "Was that a good idea?"

He shrugged. "It's not like I can answer him. So, at least this way, he'll think something's interfering with their reception."

She stared at him. "I never would have thought of doing something like that."

"And that's why I'm the one in front," he said patiently. "And you're the one who's supposed to be staying behind and keeping quiet."

She frowned at that because, of course, it was the last thing she'd been. "You have a mean streak," she announced.

He spun, stared at her in shock, and then saw the laughter on her face. He shook his head and headed off again.

It was interesting dealing with him. Outside of the horrific circumstances, she was quite enjoying herself, and how stupid was that? People were dying here. Of course she'd seen death on many levels at many times, but she hadn't seen violent sudden death like this. And yet, it wasn't really bothering her. It should.

The fact that it didn't bother her bothered her. It's something that she *should* care about. Except for the fact that these pirates obviously didn't give a damn about her or anybody else on this ship, and that made her very aware of just how limited her compassion and empathy went.

She could do an awful lot more with her life than sit here and worry about terrorists trying to kill everybody on this ship just to get at her. It was that last part that bothered her. Some doctor supposedly had failed with his treatments, so the patient's family seemed to think that she would be necessary to help that doctor.

She and Jax came to the top of the stairs, and he stopped, opened the door just a hair, and placed his ear against the opening. When he obviously didn't hear anything, he opened it a hair more and looked out. The hallway, she assumed, was empty when he stepped forward. He reached out a hand, and she grabbed it. He pulled her with him, keeping her tucked behind him and out of sight. This area appeared to be more staterooms. Which made sense. These cruise ships were just so freaking huge that they needed tons of rooms to hold their passengers, not to mention to house their employees and staff.

Jax's head tilted to the side. A sign that she now recognized as him communicating with Beau. She whispered against his head, "What's he saying?"

He held up a finger and shot her a hard look. She rolled her eyes. He grinned, leaned down, whispered against her ear, "He's taking out four more."

She wanted to laugh out loud. But instead she said, "So now you're even?"

He waited for a second, as if computing it, and then shrugged and nodded.

"They can't have too many more left," she whispered.

He nodded. "But just one remaining is too many," he said.

She agreed with that. He led her up another flight of stairs and then another. Now they were getting up to the higher levels and the more expensive suites on board. She could see the gleaming water out the windows, and yet, all that beauty held such a fake calmness to what truly went on inside. Suddenly he darted forward, checked the cabin number, opened it, and pulled her inside. He closed the door quietly, and, at the sound of a voice behind her, she gasped and turned.

There was Beau, standing with his hands on his hips. He grinned at her. "Not quite the plan you had envisioned, huh?"

She shook her head, ran a few steps, and threw herself into his arms. He chuckled and hugged her close. When she stepped back, she looked up. "I'm so glad you're okay."

He raised an eyebrow and looked from her to Jax and then back at her again. "Of course I'm okay. Why wouldn't I be?"

Abby groaned. "There's just something about being around men who are difficult."

He looked at Jax. "Number count?" Jax told him, and Beau nodded. "Same. How many more pirates do you think we've got ahead of us?"

"You'd think they'd run out soon," Jax said quietly. "But every time I turn around, there's more of them."

"Right," Abby said. "They never seem to quit, do they?"

"No. We need better intel." Beau held up four communication devices he'd taken off his pirates encountered. "These keep crackling, and I keep interfering with the reception but can't keep anybody alive long enough to question him."

"I left two alive, one should still be alive for sure," Jax said, "but they're not in any shape to talk."

Beau nodded. "What we need is to grab one and keep him prisoner and interrogate him. I think we're down to that point now." Just then he cocked his head to the side and held his finger up, then headed toward the door.

As he stepped out without a sound, she gasped and

turned toward Jax. He looked at her and shook his head, so she waited.

Within seconds, Beau returned, carrying a man, his arm around the pirate's throat as the man fought against Beau's massive size and strength and then passed out. Beau stepped into the small living area of this suite and dropped him. "Now we've got a live one," he announced.

She stared at him, walked to the closest chair, and sank down. She'd never seen anybody with such natural strength. He winked at her, and she gave him a brief smile and said, "Thanks for keeping this one alive."

He shrugged. "You're a doctor, so okay, but can't say I'm too bothered. These guys are prepared to shoot all of us just to get at you."

When the man on the ground gasped for air, Jax grabbed him by the jacket and shoved him into a chair. "Now," he said, "the only reason you're alive is so you can talk. So, talk." The man just glared at him. Jax shrugged, reached out with his fist, and gave him a light tap.

But Abby could see the blow ricocheted throughout his jaw and his skull.

When he finally could, the pirate gasped and said, "Stop." He looked at Abby and whispered, "You won't let them do this, will you?"

"How many men did you shoot and kill already today?" she asked quietly. "How many innocent passengers have died for whatever bloody cause you think you're after?"

Obviously he understood what she was saying and knew that he didn't have much of an answer. He glanced from one man to the other. "What do you want to know?"

"How many men are here with you?"

He shrugged. "There were twenty-three of us. The big

boss, his two leaders, and then twenty of us soldiers."

"And where are they all?"

"That's what we're trying to figure out," he said. "We're not getting good reception here, and so I've been sent to make sure everybody's in position."

Jax pointed to the fourteen communication devices gathered in one corner. Beau held up another five. The pirate's gaze went from the devices back to Beau and back down to the corner again, and his eyes widened. "Did you kill them all?"

Beau shrugged. "Anybody who wants to fight me can, but I don't guarantee results."

The man swallowed visibly. "Sixteen are supposedly in the bowels of the ship. Four are up top with the team leads and the boss."

"Who's the boss?" she asked curiously. "Apparently he's looking for me."

He nodded. "The boss's nephew is dying. And the boy's doctor says that he can't do what he needs to do and that he needs you."

She stared at him. "And what difference does it make if I'm there or not?"

"I don't know," he said. "But because the doc says he needs you, the boss will do everything he can to get you."

"Who's the doctor?" Jax asked in a hard voice.

"Dr. Benjamin Windberg," he said.

She stared at the pirate, but inside she was reeling. She wanted to vomit and scream at the same time.

Jax reached for her, pulling her close. "Do you know him?"

She nodded faintly. "Yes," she said. "He was always a problem."

"Why?"

"He attended med school with me," she murmured, hating to even talk about this man. "He stalked me. Sent me nasty notes. It started off nice, friendly, and then, all of a sudden, he told everyone that he was supposedly my lover, and I wasn't allowed to have friends. I ended up getting a court injunction, and he left the country ahead of the cops." She reached up a shaky hand and pushed away the tendrils of hair that whispered around her face. "Why would he do this?"

"Revenge?" Beau offered.

"It's possible." She nodded. "He was very fixated on me back then."

"So this is all just a ruse to get to you?" Jax asked, his tone rising. "Or do you think there really is a sick boy?"

She stared at the gunman. "Is that what this is?"

He just shrugged and said, "As far as our boss is concerned, it's all about keeping his nephew alive. Because his doctor says he needs you, then he needs you. If you have a history with the doctor, I don't know anything about it. But I hope, for my sake, that you can do whatever needs to be done because it'll just be bad news for the doctor and everyone else if the boss's only nephew dies."

She sighed, looked at the other two men, and said, "I don't know what to say."

"I don't know either," Jax said. "What do you want to do?"

"I want these guys to stop killing everybody," she cried out. "I want to know that the passengers are all safe."

He glanced at the prisoner. "Any chance your boss will be reasonable?"

The soldier shook his head. "No. It's his nephew. His

only nephew. He's got five nieces, but this is his only nephew."

"What's wrong with the nephew?" she asked.

"Some blood disease. He was too sick for the treatment to work or something. Cancer, I think," he said, "but I don't know what kind."

"What age?" When the pirate didn't know, she fired off more questions that she needed answers to, in order to fully understand what the patient's condition was. Even though this man had passed along some generic information, how could she believe him? She wondered how he was privy to *any* insider information, so had to doubt the veracity of his words.

"I don't know if I can even help him. I must see him for myself."

Jax made a decisive headshake and said, "Not in this lifetime."

⚓

JAX WASN'T SURE what was going on, but adding in the personal element between the two doctors was a whole different story. He glared at the prisoner. "And who is this boss man?"

He named somebody Jax had never heard of. He glanced at Beau, who studied their captive intently. "He's one of the sheikh's cousins, isn't he?"

The gunman nodded. "He's a very wealthy man, and he holds a lot of power within our country."

"Where is his nephew currently?"

"In a private holding outside of Dubai," he said.

"Ah," she said, "that would make sense. The *good* Dr.

Windberg intended on going back there."

"Is he from there?" Jax asked.

She shrugged. "I'm not exactly sure where he was from, but I met him in the States and do know you can't trust anything he says."

"How bad was it between the two of you?" He watched the muscles in her face and in her jaw tense and then flickered, as she stressed out over trying to answer him. Finally he nodded and said, "Did he get his hands on you?"

She gave him the ghost of a smile and said, "Not for long."

He nodded. "Good." He turned to look at his prisoner. "Is the doctor here?"

The prisoner shook his head. "No, he's not. He's waiting in Dubai to take her."

"And you're just supposed to hand her over like that?"

The gunman shrugged. "It's not for me to know," he complained. "The boss is running the show."

"And the boss is here?"

"He's also the head of security and the uncle of the sick boy."

"Okay, so let me get this straight," Beau said. "This man's son is dying, so he hires the doctor. The doctor says he needs this second doctor. So the father sends brother, who is also his head of security—the big boss, as you called him—onto this cruise ship with two of his teams of men."

The pirate nodded. "Yes," and then he fell silent.

"In which case, we should pretty well have taken out all the lower-level soldiers," Jax said. He glanced down at their captive. "How do I tell the two top dogs from the head of security here?"

"The two are in blue uniforms," he said.

Jax nodded. "Well, one of them is dead."

The man sucked in his breath and paled. "Please don't kill me. I'm just doing a job, like everybody else. We were trying to save our boss's nephew."

"In a very devious manner," she said. "I believe you about the man's son. The rest just makes no sense. Surely there had to be other ways to contact me. Even to kidnap me. But the fact is, you were prepared to kill hundreds of passengers to get me."

"Of course," he said, "it's the way we do things."

She winced. Jax looked over a Beau and said, "Plans?"

Beau made a decisive nod.

And his fist connected with the side of the man's head. The gunman slumped over, unconscious.

CHAPTER 7

ABBY JUMPED TO her feet, ran over, and checked that he was still breathing. Then she turned on Beau, fisting her hands on her hips and glaring up at him.

"Hey, I didn't kill him," he said.

She groaned but gave him points for his restraint. "So now what?"

"I figure we've got one more pirate on the loose, one more top dog to find and the big boss," Jax said.

"My best guess is that they should be up on the topmost deck with whatever passengers they're holding prisoner," Beau said. "Or with the captain and his crew."

"In which case, why don't I talk to them?" she asked.

"And what will you say?"

"I'll tell him the truth about the doctor and that I'd be happy to look after his nephew, but I will not travel to his country to see him."

Both men stopped and stared at her. "You would treat the boy after all this?"

She raised her eyebrows and said, "The nephew isn't responsible, is he?"

The two men looked at each other, frowned.

"We'd need a neutral location, somewhere closer to Dubai, since the boy's condition seems really bad."

Jax stared at her. "You do realize Windberg will be there,

as the physician for the nephew, right?"

She shrugged.

"But we'll keep him separated from you."

Again she shrugged. "I don't care where the hospital is," she said. "Pick a country. We must get the boy to a decent hospital, and I need privileges at that hospital."

The men looked at each other. Jax pulled out his cell phone, made a call, and, as soon as Griffin answered on the other end, Jax explained the problem.

"I'm not sure what we can organize fast enough to treat what may be a dying boy," Griffin said. "I agree. She can't go to Dubai. Chances are, she'll never leave."

"The other problem is," Jax said, "make sure that Dr. Windberg isn't allowed to get his hands on her."

"Good point. You're sure you only have three more men left to take down?"

"No," Jax said. "I'm definitely not sure of that. It could be any number because you can't ever trust what a prisoner says."

"You could ask him again," Griffin said, but the note of humor in his voice meant he already knew that the man couldn't answer.

Abby wasn't sure what to think about all this, but the men had taken charge yet again, and so things were happening. She didn't know if it would entail everybody on board or whether the guys would fly her out and arrange for a meeting somewhere else. But somehow she'd been embroiled in a much deeper scenario. She had no problem trying to help the man's nephew, but she couldn't guarantee the boy's cure either.

She needed a whole lot more details. Knowing Dr. Windberg was involved, it must deal with her specialty, stem cells. She could possibly do a stem-cell transfer for the boy, which could have miraculous results in some cases, but there was no guarantee that it would solve whatever the boy suffered from. Depending on the nephew's age and his overall constitution, any other medical conditions could be impacting all that. She sat here, thinking about what she would do. She looked at Jax and said, "Any other doctor would do in this scenario to help the boy. You know that, right?"

He shook his head. "Not if the child's doctor has the father convinced that the only way his son will live is if you're brought on board," he said gently. "You know what families are like when a loved one is in jeopardy."

She nodded. "Unfortunately I do know all too well. Still, any decent hospital should be able to help him."

"And so," Beau said, "we find a hospital that will take the boy and you, keeping your part of the bargain."

"Unfortunately," Jax said, "we're caught up in a mess where the rules are very different."

"I know," she said sadly. "I wish the rest of the world was nicer."

"I wish all the world would be much nicer," Jax said in a harsh tone. "But *nice* means nothing in today's day and age of murdering people for no reason."

"So what will we do? Maybe find a hospital in England? I do have several colleagues there who are very good at what they do."

Both men looked at her with interest. "That's possible. If we could get the boy and you there, we could work with MI6 on this to ensure that you're safe."

She nodded. "And potentially pick up Dr. Windberg for his part in these murders," she said slowly. "Because I think he had some British … I'm not saying *citizenship*, but maybe a residency?" She shook her head. "I'm not exactly sure what his relationship was with the UK government, but I know he felt quite comfortable working and living over there."

"Even better," Jax said, "but somebody still has to come to some arrangement with the remaining pirates on board."

"And that'll be our next problem to resolve," Beau said.

As he spoke, the door slammed open, and three gunmen screamed at them in a foreign tongue, guns drawn and pointing at each of them.

Shocked, Abby bolted into Jax's arms. He quickly shoved her behind him, but there was nothing for it. Jax and Beau couldn't get to their guns fast enough under these circumstances. Plus they had to consider Abby. She couldn't be around gunfire.

Finally Beau, with his hands in the air, asked, "Do you speak English?"

One of the men, dressed in blue, straightened and nodded and said, "Yes. Who are you?"

"Friends of the doctor," he said, pointing to Abby.

Jax stared at the gunman who spoke to them and said, "And I'm her husband."

The three pirates glared at her. "Our intel doesn't say she was married."

"Your intel is wrong," she snapped, her head poking out from under Jax's arm and around his back. "Why are you doing this?"

The third man stepped forward. He glared at them and said to Abby, "You are coming with us."

The big boss, Jax guessed.

She frowned and said, "You kill passengers on a cruise ship because of one little boy?"

His frown deepened, then he shrugged. "I don't care about the other passengers. That little boy is all I care about."

She pinched the bridge of her nose because she'd heard it time and time again. "Then we'll reach a compromise," she said slowly. "I'm not coming to Dubai. Your Dr. Windberg," she said, "doesn't want me to help that boy but wants me for himself."

The armed pirates glared at her. "How dare you insult our esteemed doctor!" said the pirate in the blue uniform.

Just then Beau shook his head and said, "You're not listening. This is all documented in the US police files. This man has tried to hurt her several times. He doesn't want her there to help look after the little boy. He wants her there for himself."

The big boss nodded to the man in blue, who studied the three Americans, but his frowned deepened. "I must make a call." And he stepped back. They could hear him talking in a rapid-fire voice out in the hallway. But the other two gunmen didn't move.

This, then, were likely the three remaining pirates. At least she hoped there were no others.

When the man returned, he glared at them and said, "We need you to look after this little boy."

"And I'm willing to look at him," she said quietly. "I can't guarantee that I can fix whatever's wrong with him, but I'm not willing to go as your prisoner. I'll meet him in England at this hospital." She named the specific hospital that she wanted the patient at. At least she hoped she could get him admitted there.

He shook his head immediately.

She shrugged. "Then kill me now."

He looked at her in shock.

She nodded. "I'm not going to Dubai. I won't be Dr. Windberg's prisoner. I won't be tormented and tortured by him anymore."

So much passion and outrage were evident in her voice that the pirate studied her for a long time. "You really believe that Dr. Windberg doesn't want you there for professional reasons?"

"I know perfectly well he doesn't want me there for professional reasons," she said. "Maybe out of revenge, maybe out of jealousy, maybe out of an obsession that's gone terribly wrong. So shoot me now or meet me in London, and I will try to help the little boy there."

He motioned at the two men with the rifles. "They will kill you now."

She stepped forward and kept on walking until she had the blue-uniformed man's rifle against her chest. She looked at the gunman and said, "Shoot me then."

Silence filled the room.

⚓

JAX COULDN'T BELIEVE what she'd just done. Not only did it take guts, but it also took grit. But he didn't dare take his eyes off her. It could all go to shit right now. But, if they shot her, he would take out the shooter and make sure that neither of these men ever had a chance to take a breath again.

The gunman stared at her in shock. He turned his head, looking at his boss for orders. Because, if the boss said to shoot, then what? And that's when this would go south very quickly.

Jax hadn't expected her to not only walk into the barrel of the pirate's gun but to push the issue right past maximum. He knew that Beau's breath was caught in his throat too, when neither one of them dared to say anything. The bloodbath was about to happen, but, while all eyes were on her, Jax slid his hand slightly to his back and pulled a handgun free. Now he just needed the right moment.

As far as he was concerned, you take out the top dog, and the men below became rudderless. Then he might make a trip to Dubai and take care of a certain doctor all on his own. If they could get him to England, well, Jax would enlist all the help he could get to make sure that asshole doctor went down for as much of this murder plot as could be laid at his feet. Obviously this guy hadn't changed his colors just because he'd left the country.

As Jax watched, the boss man shook his head, and a heavy discussion ensued. And, not for the first time, Jax wished he spoke Arabic.

By the time the discussion was over, the gunman in blue lowered the rifle against Abby and said, "You will come with us."

She smiled at him gently and said, "No, I won't."

One of the pirates grabbed her and tugged her toward the doorway. Jax lifted his handgun and put a bullet between his eyes. She immediately dropped to the ground, and the other gunman in blue hit the ground too, dead now, courtesy of Beau's bullet. But the pirate in blue got one shot off before he died, or maybe a reflex action happened as the bullet hit him. Either way, his stray bullet hit the pirate they had just questioned.

Now, with both Beau and Jax holding weapons on the leader, the big boss glared at them and spat, "And now what?

You'll shoot me too?"

"None of you would've died," Abby said, bouncing to her feet, "if you'd just let me go."

He shook his head. "Then we would be dead when we go home. A bullet is much faster."

"Go home and tell the father that I'll meet him and the boy at the hospital in London," she said quietly. "The boy doesn't deserve this. The father does. But the boy doesn't."

The boss man looked at her in surprise.

She nodded. "You get every last man of yours off this ship right now, and I will meet the little boy in England. And, if there are any more attempts made on my life or the lives of the men with me or the lives of these passengers, that little boy doesn't get a chance in hell."

His face darkened at her threat.

She shook her head. "No. You've threatened thousands of lives here," she snapped. "No more games. I'm happy to use my medical expertise to help the boy. *If I can.* No guarantees, no miracles. But, if there's anything I can do to help, I will. But I'm not willing to go back and deal with Dr. Windberg. He's a criminal. He's a sadist, and he's a rapist of women. And I will have nothing to do with him."

At her words, he stiffened. "I must tell my boss."

"Why don't you let me speak to him?"

He frowned. His phone was still in his hand. He hit Dial, spoke into it, and then handed it over.

"This is Dr. Abigail Eleanor," she said crisply. "I'm sending all your men home. If you want me to consult on your son's medical problem, I'll meet him at the London hospital of my choosing on Tuesday afternoon, UK time, to allow for time zone differences and travel arrangements to be made. But Dr. Windberg is not to be anywhere around me. He's a rapist, not allowed in the States. And I will be happy to inform MI6 of this as well. So, if you make any more attempts on my life or anybody on this cruise liner or anybody in my vicinity, I'll make sure your son doesn't ever take another breath."

And she hung up. She tossed the pirate his phone and said, "Now gather your men and leave."

He looked down at the three in this area, all visibly dead, and looked at the two men standing behind her and said, "You might as well just throw them overboard. I can't take them off here."

She raised her eyebrows. "Is that how you look after your dead?"

He shrugged. "They were hired men. It's the way of the world."

"Don't they have families?"

"Yes, but I don't know who they are."

"Give me an address in Saudi Arabia," she said. "Preferably Dubai, where we can deliver the corpses."

He frowned, pulled out his phone, brought up something, and held up the address for her. She took a photo of it. When she was done, he asked, "Why would you do that?"

"Well, I could say something nasty, like we don't want corpses floating in our seas or rotting on our lands," she said. "But the fact of the matter is, their bodies should be disposed of with dignity. They fought on the wrong side. They took money for a job that had no semblance of goodwill behind it. Yet, I can't find myself capable of throwing them overboard."

"Talk to the men behind you," he said with a half-smile. "They'd have no problem doing so."

"No. These are honorable men who do the right thing,

even for pirates who attacked this ship," she said steadily. "My current concern is that you and anybody left alive of your crew immediately retreat and stop this senseless killing."

He stood, looked at her and at his men on the floor, and said, "Depending on how many you've taken out, there is likely only me left."

"You've got a five-minute head start then," Jax said in a hard voice behind her. "And then I'm coming after you."

He shot him a baleful look, and, in the next second, he was gone.

Abby slowly turned to him and said, "Jesus, is this over yet?"

"No," he said, walking forward gently. He put his arms around her, tucked her up close, and said, "Are you sure about Tuesday? Given it's already Saturday, and we have yet to properly dispose of the bodies, plus our travel time, and the loss of hours due to the time zone change …"

She nodded. "I am sure. But we must make sure that the captain and all the rest of the crew are okay, and maybe we can get some normality returned here." She looked at the two men. "And we must collect all the dead men before we leave."

Jax pulled out his phone, checked for the number he needed, hit Dial, and, as soon as Griffin came on, he said, "Patch me through to the cruise ship captain."

Griffin gave a half a snort and said, "Hang on."

A new voice was on the other end. "Who is this?" asked a man, anger and frustration in his voice.

"I'm Jax Darrum," Jax said. "I'm on your cruise ship, and we've taken charge, taking out twenty-two pirates. One more pirate is leaving the ship intact, of his own free will, but we need to store a lot of bodies until we can get them moved off."

"Who are you?" asked the captain in a disbelieving tone. "And how many of you are there?"

"We are special ops. There are two of us," Jax said calmly, adding in their suite number. "Where do you want the bodies?"

"In the kitchen cooler," he said. "I don't know what else to do. We don't exactly have a morgue on board."

"But you have a medical bay, right?"

"Yes," he said, "but only as a temporary holding area to make arrangements to unload bodies. And then it is only designed to hold one or two."

"I think I can help with that," he said. "But we need some strong men to give us a hand."

"They'll be right there."

His phone went dead. He turned, looked at Abby, and smiled. "The captain is sending some men down."

"And do we believe him? Do we trust him? Is there any chance that he's involved?"

Jax's eyebrows popped up. "Wow, you've become such an untrusting soul."

She snorted. "I was never very trusting to begin with. And that asshole doctor went a long way to making my life miserable. I don't trust anything he's mixed up in."

"In that case," Beau said, "why are you meeting these guys in London? You can't confirm the boy is ill."

She looked at him in surprise. "Because it's what I do. I'm known for being a specialist in blood diseases."

Jax nodded. "Which explains why they went to such great lengths to get you."

"It doesn't mean they'll still meet me in London though," she said quietly. "Or that England will allow us all in."

"We'll set that up too, but with added security."

She gave him a ghost of a smile. "Okay. It's my job, when I get there, to see the boy. It's your job to get me there safe and sound and to keep everybody else safe while it's happening," she said cheerfully. He just stared at her. She shrugged. "I know you like a challenge."

Jax shook his head. "There are challenges, and then there are suicide missions. What you just did a few minutes ago? Now *that* was a suicide mission."

"Like the guy said," she said, the fatigue showing up in her voice now, "a bullet is faster than what that doctor would have had me suffer through."

"Is he really that twisted?" Beau asked.

She nodded. "He's really that twisted."

CHAPTER 8

As soon as the call was done, she looked at Jax and said, "What do I do now?"

"Well, it'll be a bit of a clean-up mess," he said. "We'll collect all the bodies, and then the captain will make an announcement to all aboard the ship."

"Well, the captain is right here," said a man in a white uniform. He looked at Jax, looked at Beau, and then at her. "I presume you're the doctor for whom everybody was hunting?"

She nodded. "I'm sorry. I had no idea this was even going on."

"Well, I'm not sure who these gentlemen with you are, but I'm glad it's all over." He held out his hand to the two men. "You have my thanks."

Both men nodded, and shook his hand, then Jax asked, "Did you bring us some men?"

He nodded.

Jax stepped out to see six men in the hallway and said, "I need three with me and three with Beau to collect the bodies and prisoners."

"Any idea how many?"

Jax looked at the captain and said, "Twenty-two pirates and four passengers, I believe."

The captain winced and said, "Obviously this has been a

very lucky day for the rest of us."

"In some cases, yes," Jax said.

The captain looked at Jax and said, "Before I make an announcement to the passengers, I'll give you an hour to collect and move the bodies. I don't want the passengers to see all this carnage."

"We've stashed the pirates' weapons into multiple places as well."

Abby groaned. "I forgot all about those. A whole arsenal is in the women's washroom several floors down." The captain raised his eyebrows, and she shrugged. "We had to take them off those who we took out, just in case."

Jax turned to the captain, nudging Abby closer. "I ask that you keep her with you up in your cabin. We think we have every hostile accounted for, but I don't want to take any chances."

The captain immediately nodded and motioned to her. "Come. Follow me. Let these men do their job."

She turned to look back at Jax and said, "And remember they may not all be dead."

He smiled and said, "Not your problem, Doc."

She gave him a good frown and said, "Why is that?"

"Because a medical facility is on board, and it's fully staffed," he said gently. "You're off duty until Tuesday."

Abby paused, nodded, and said, "Sounds good."

Jax separated the men off, three of them handling the three dead just in this room, and said, "Two teams, let's go downstairs."

And they were off.

And Abby turned and followed the captain up to his quarters, which he pointed out to her, and then took Abby to the top deck to take a look at what was happening there.

Several men bounced to attention when they saw the captain, and then they looked at her. Their eyebrows popped up, and she smiled and introduced herself. Then she added, "The ship is safe now."

At that, the sighs of relief were visible across their faces.

"Seriously?" asked one of the men.

The captain said, "Yes, we believe so. There's a chance that we're still missing one, but we have several teams now heading off and gathering up the bodies and the weapons that have been sprawled across our ship. We're giving them an hour. Then we'll do a full announcement and get the ship back to normal."

"Wow." The men sat down and looked at each other, with expressions somewhere between relief and fear. The anxiety had taken its toll.

Abby looked at the captain and said, "I'm not sure where your supplies are, but I'm pretty sure everybody will benefit from good food and maybe some free booze to help lighten their souls."

He snorted. "That'll be the least of our problems. Obviously we'll do something in order to make this memory a whole lot easier on our guests. But the cruise company will decide how to handle that from here on in."

She nodded. "And I'll need a place to crash soon too. Now that the adrenaline has worn off, I'm afraid I'm more than slightly exhausted."

He nodded in understanding. "You can have my quarters in my office. A couch is in there."

She smiled and thanked him and said, "We'll wait until this is all over with, and then maybe I'll sleep."

"Can you tell us anything about what happened?" asked one of the men beside her.

She shrugged. "Apparently a man in Dubai is a relative to one of the sheikhs," she said with a bit of an eye roll. "His son is quite sick, and his doctor said they needed me and my services to save the son."

There was silence for a moment. "Why you?" asked another of the men hesitantly.

She gave him a cheeky grin and said, "You know what? That's a very good question, but I think it's because the other doctor knows me." And she left it at that. But the men appeared to be in much better spirits, and, when coffee was finally delivered, and a bottle of whiskey was brought out, everybody enjoyed a shot as they cheered on having their lives back again.

By the time all the pirates had been collected, apparently all of them dead now, she was beyond exhausted. The captain had given her his office and a couch to lie down on. The captain stayed and worked, but then, as if realizing he was disturbing her, he'd gotten up. She protested and said that, as far as she was concerned, he could stay. She didn't really want to be alone. But he shook his head.

"No," he said. "You obviously need sleep. I don't want to impact that. And you aren't alone as we will be in shouting distance. It's been a very harrowing day for all of us."

"As soon as Jax gets back," she said, "I want to know."

"I'll send him in when he returns," the captain said. And, with a smile, he turned and walked out.

⚓

JAX HATED TO wake her. Even though it was hours later, she was bound to be exhausted, but they had lots more traveling to come. He could give her another hour, but that was it. He'd already arranged with the captain for an airlift off the cruise liner for the three of them, but they had to get a little closer to shore first. That rendezvous would take place in just over an hour. An hour and fifteen, according to his watch. The local coast guard had already arrived to remove the weapons and the bodies. Jax, Beau, and Abby had all given their statements to the captain, who shared them with the coast guard, who would then share them again at the request of any other authorities. So at least she'd already taken care of that ordeal.

From here, they would head to the mainland via the airlift, should arrive midafternoon or later, and, with any luck, would be at the international airport soon enough to grab the last Saturday afternoon jet to England. He was hoping to get her to a hotel soon enough so that they could crash, handle any jet lag, and get some real sleep tonight—before they set up the security details with the hospital and with MI6 for the upcoming meeting.

MI6 had been flabbergasted that she even wanted to meet with the father and son duo and hadn't been impressed that she had chosen their home turf for such a meeting. However, when Jax had explained who this doctor to a well-known Arab family was and why Abby thought maybe Dr. Windberg would be allowed into the hospital, they perked up and said, "We have a big, thick file on him."

"Why?" Jax asked.

"Various issues," they said but wouldn't elaborate.

Jax frowned on that. He'd asked Griffin to get more information on this Dr. Windberg as well. Jax wouldn't go into anything blind, and no way would he let Abby go into this blind.

Finally it was time to wake her. He walked into the captain's room, and, as soon as he opened the door and stepped in, immediately Abby opened her eyes and looked at him bleary-eyed.

He smiled and said, "You've got about five minutes to wake up. Then we'll start the first leg of our journey to England."

She groaned. "Fine. Can't say I'm thrilled though."

He reached out a hand, and she stood slowly and then winced.

"Are you hurt?"

"No, just sore," she said. "Involved in a lot of activities I wasn't used to lately."

"To be expected," he said. "If nothing else, the stress can cause your body to lock into different positions. But we need to go, and we aren't stopping until we hit London. And it'll be late Sunday when we do. So let's go grab your personal belongings and get started."

And he meant it. They made their Saturday late-afternoon flight—luckily—and settled in for a long seventeen-hour transatlantic flight. Then, allowing for the time zone differences, it was now nine p.m., Sunday evening, as they finally reached their hotel in London just a few blocks away from the designated hospital. Jax led her through the numbered hotel door and said, "This is your room."

She spun around to look at him, her eyebrows shooting up. "You mean, I get some privacy?"

"Well, you get a little bit of it," he said. "It's a suite, and Beau and I'll share the bedroom across the living room."

She turned and nodded. "Okay. That makes more sense." Then she sighed. "I just want to shower and crash. And I don't want to sleep too long," she said, yawning. "But

I need enough to make it through the rest of the day."

"It isn't daytime anymore. We're heading to bed. So, it's either order food now or wait until morning."

She thought about it and said, "How about I shower, and, in the meantime, you can order up something from room service? I'll eat and then go to bed."

"Done," he said. He closed the door gently behind her and headed over to talk to Beau, grabbing up the room service menu as he went. They quickly placed an order and were told it would take about forty minutes. At that, they both had time to take a shower, so Jax jumped in first, came out shortly thereafter, set up their laptops, and began a plan for the next two days.

"We should check in with MI6," Beau said. "Although they likely know we're already here."

"Wish we didn't have to," Jax said.

"We're pissing in their backyard," Beau said. "I highly doubt we can come and go without raising some kind of a major issue."

"It's Dr. Windberg who will flag all kinds of issues. We need to let him into the country just so MI6 can pick him up."

"And, for that, you must talk to MI6." Leaving that duty to Jax, Beau grabbed a shower.

Jax snorted and pulled out his phone, then sent Griffin a request for a MI6 contact. His phone rang instantly. *Griffin.*

"His name is Jonas."

"You could have waited until tomorrow," Jax said in exasperation.

"With MI6, you really want them to be in on it at the beginning," he said. "They get their noses out of joint and make life difficult otherwise."

"But we're waiting for food, and she needs to sleep."

"Got it," Griffin said. "I'm sending you a bunch of files. I've got several links for you to take a look at as well. This doctor is an interesting character."

"Files on what?" Jax asked, walking to his laptop and bringing up his email and downloading the files. The Mavericks chat box popped up with a series of links. He opened them in different tabs.

"History on Dr. Benjamin Windberg and history on the father, Nahim, and son, Abdul, and Nahim's brother, Bahan."

"How do we know this is the sick boy?" he asked, studying the obviously sick youngster held in some man's arms.

"The doctor has made no bones about who it is he works for. He's touting himself as a specialist in Dubai."

"They'll lynch him if he kills that little boy," Jax said.

"He won't see it coming either," Griffin said. "But his ego is by far bigger than his sense of danger."

"MI6 says they have a thick file on him. Can you get the contents for us? They wouldn't say anything earlier."

"Good question," Griffin said, his voice distracted. "Let me work on that. They aren't normally cooperative. So maybe not. I might be able to get a look at it and see if there is anything we don't already know."

And they hung up. Jax put the phone beside him and searched through the files he did have, looking for anything that would help him understand the obsessive nature and the why behind the doctor who had gone after Abby. Obviously she was gorgeous and cute and smart and funny and courageous and full of grit and all those things that he didn't think the doctor would really appreciate. She had a figure to die for, and that might be the part of her that most intrigued

Windberg. Yet something about the whole package got to Jax.

But what was it exactly that got to the doctor? Maybe his ego at work again, refusing to give up on her. Or the alternative side of that same flaming overblown ego—his first attempt had failed. Jax didn't think this Windberg guy would deal well with failure.

When Abby came out in a hotel robe, her hair pulled back with her face scrubbed clean, she looked like she was all of eighteen years old.

He smiled and said, "That getup doesn't do anything to age you."

"Drat," she said. "And here I was hoping to look at least my twenty-nine years."

"No," he said, "definitely a decade younger than that."

She smiled, curled up in the corner of the couch, and said, "At least I have clothes. I'll get changed in a little bit, but I'm so tired I just want to put on my pajamas."

"Can't you eat in pajamas?"

The look on her face was one he hadn't seen before, and her tone was dry when she said, "No, not these ones."

Immediately his mind spun to see-through lingerie or tiny, itsy-bitsy pieces that didn't cover anything.

He gave a hard shake of his head and said, "Don't put images like that in some guy's head. It'll get you in trouble."

"Depends if it's trouble I want," she said, stifling a yawn. She sagged against the couch and said, "Really wouldn't matter tonight. I'm so tired that I'd probably just sleep anyway."

Jax gave a bark of laughter. "Well, you might cut it short, but I can't imagine you ever sleeping through it."

She shot him a grin. "So that means you're a better lover

than the ones I've been with, presumably."

He stopped, stared, and said, "Seriously? You haven't slept through sex, have you?"

Her lighthearted laughter filled the room. "No. I tend to view sex as a participation activity, not something I sit on the sidelines and watch."

He swore softly as more images slid seductively through his way-too-wild imagination. "We're sidelining this conversation. You look way too cute and adorable in that outfit for me to even go down that train of thought."

"Why?" she asked with interest. But the twinkle in her gaze had him turning away.

"Oh no," he said. "I know how that teasing starts."

"Well, I can get dressed if you want," she said, "but I can't say that that's terribly appealing."

"Don't worry about it," he said. "Beau is in the shower right now. When he's out, hopefully we'll have food."

"As long as nobody else is coming," she said, "I don't care."

At that, he looked up at her and said, "Quite possibly we will have visitors."

She bolted to her feet. "In that case, I'm getting dressed."

"Don't get dressed on my account," he said. "I really like the view."

"Ha," she said. "But do you want other men seeing that view?"

And the door shut quietly in his face.

Good point, he thought to himself. The answer to that was, no way did he want anybody else to see her like this. She was adorable in many, many ways, but she was also somebody he'd come to greatly admire. She hadn't broken down in tears once during this whole ordeal; she hadn't had a fit of hysteria at seeing dead bodies, both the pirates' and the passengers'. She hadn't fainted when he had killed several men in front of her, and neither had she blanched nor run away from the violence or what was asked of her. She'd stepped up each and every time. Especially when daring the pirates to kill her for not doing as they said, standing her ground with them. Twice. He shook his head. Scary shit, but that was something he could respect too.

When Beau stepped out, his hair was slicked back and wet, but he looked a whole lot better. His friend said, "I'd really like to know what put that look on your face."

Jax just shrugged and stared at him, deliberately keeping his gaze off the bedroom door beside them.

But Beau nodded. "There really is something between the two of you, isn't there?"

"Nope," Jax said. "In different circumstances, maybe. But this one, absolutely not."

"That's because you're too professional to take a sideline trip like that," Beau said. "But you also must realize that you should act when the opportunity is there."

"Again, shitty timing," Jax said.

"Agreed."

On that note she stepped from her room in capris and a T-shirt this time. And, if she thought it would look any less revealing, she was wrong because the capris were stretchy and hugged her hips and tiny waist. And even though she didn't have long legs, what there were of them were extremely shapely. And the T-shirt clung in all the right places. He deliberately returned his gaze to his laptop and tried hard to focus. But it was damn difficult. She had curves bursting in all the right places, and his hands were just itching to cup and slide and explore every one of them. He was saved from an embarrassing moment when a hard knock came at the door.

She instinctively raced toward him. "Any way to know who that is?" she whispered.

"Don't need to know," he said. "That's MI6. I was hoping our food would arrive first, but we aren't so lucky."

"We didn't order enough for them, did we?"

He gave a bark of laughter. "No, they can get their own." He walked over, checked the peephole, and then threw open the door. He looked at the man, MI6 all the way from the suit to the wingtips. Then he held out his hand and said, "Jonas, I believe."

Jonas nodded, shook his hand, and said, "Jonas Halpern, at your service." He glanced into the rest of the room. "How many are you? And how soon are you leaving? It can't be fast enough for my liking. Do you Americans do anything but cause trouble?"

"Just Beau and I and, of course, Dr. Eleanor."

Jonas stepped inside, closed the door quietly, and said, "Are you trying to stay low?"

"We'll do our best," Beau said. "But obviously we've both been tagged through security already."

"Indeed, you have," he said. "Partly why I'm here. I understand it's got something to do with our doctor here. But you're also bringing in another criminal and a very sick boy. We need an explanation for those."

At that, Abby piped up and said, "We're not trying to cause any trouble, but I admit that Dr. Windberg and Abdul's father do make things happen and not always pleasantly."

He studied her for a long moment, then reached out and

shook her hand. "Pleased to meet you. Your reputation precedes you."

She shrugged. "Don't know why it would have," she said. "But I'm okay as long as it's all good things."

"Well, it was until you arranged for this little boy to come here onto our doorstep."

"I was trying to get out of a very difficult situation," she said. "And the sins of the fathers don't necessarily slide down to the children. And, if I can help the boy, I will. But that Dr. Windberg …" She shook her head. "He needs to be put away."

"And yet, you want him in our country," Jonas said. "How are we supposed to reconcile that?"

"Well, I was hoping you'd catch him, incarcerate him. He's a criminal. I just don't know to what extent, outside of his harassment of me."

"And what has he done wrong?"

Jax watched a neutral look settle on Jonas's face.

She quickly explained, and Jonas frowned. "So why isn't he in jail in the US?"

"Because he shipped out first," she said.

"So you're hoping that he'll do something wrong here, and we can snag him and throw him into our jail at our taxpayers' expense?"

"I don't know what other crimes he may have committed, but I'm sure you'd be more aware of all that than I would," she said. "Besides, if he went after the Queen, you'd arrest him in a heartbeat."

"Maybe," he said, "but that doesn't mean that you'll be given the same consideration."

Just then another knock came on the door.

Jonas turned to look at Jax, but he was already at the

door, checking the peephole. When he opened the door, a trolley was pushed in from room service. He quickly took it, tipped the server, and closed the door before the employee could even see who was inside the hotel room. Jax brought the food over beside the table and apologized to Jonas. "We've been traveling steadily for most of the last two days. We wanted to get a meal and then go to bed."

"At least that was my plan," Abby said. She looked at the men. "You guys can stay up if you want, but I'm done."

"Understood," Jonas said. "But maybe it's better that way. We have plans to make."

Immediately she glared at him. "Meaning that, you'd be better off making the plans without me?"

Enough disbelief and outrage were in her voice that he immediately said, "No, not at all. But making plans when you're exhausted is not good either." As a backtrack, it was weak, and he knew it.

Jax chuckled. "I wouldn't try to pull anything over her. She isn't exactly a dumb bunny."

"No, I'm not," she snapped in exasperation. "And, even if I were, I wouldn't take kindly to being called that."

Jax rolled his eyes. "An intricate game of chess is involved, which takes time. Sit down and eat. You're obviously getting hungry."

She snorted at that too, but she let him get away with it. As soon as they were seated, she looked at Jonas. "I don't think we ordered enough for you."

"That's fine," he said. "I'm not hungry. But, if there's coffee, that would be good." When pointed in the right direction, he walked to the corner where a small coffeemaker sat and quickly put on a pot.

Meanwhile Jax served the food and soon had her eating.

"I still don't understand," Jonas said, "why you chose this country. You should have gone to Dubai. Kept the doctor there."

"But then I wouldn't have gotten out of Dubai, now would I?" she snapped.

Jax looked at her and raised an eyebrow.

She groaned. "Look. I'm sorry, but I'm pretty tired of all this."

"Understood," Jonas said. "At the same time, I must come up with some justification for my own government as to why this is happening."

"Oh," she said. Obviously she didn't realize what problems the country itself had to consider. "Well, sorry if that'll cause you an issue," she said, "but I didn't know what else to do. Besides I'm sure some British citizens were on that cruise ship at the time the pirates took over, killing some of the passengers. Won't that work in our favor?"

He frowned at that and then shrugged. "I can try that angle. But it won't be about saving those citizens because they should be home already. But maybe getting the man behind it all, yes." At that, he appeared satisfied.

Abby dug into her food and ignored him.

Jax felt a little bit better himself, and Beau had been very quiet but had pulled his plate of food toward him and ate at an impressive rate. Finally the two men were done, but she still worked on hers. Jax looked at Jonas and asked, "Have you got security in place, or do we take care of it ourselves?"

"We'll double up security at the hospital," Jonas said. "We'd like to talk with the father who orchestrated the takeover of the cruise ship."

"I thought you didn't want anything to do with him," she said.

"We don't, but if he's coming here on our turf, then we do."

"He probably wants clear passage to the hospital, but I wouldn't be at all surprised if he somehow diverts his plane to another location and can't make it in time," she said caustically.

"Why?" Jax asked at the same time as Jonas.

"Could be another move by Dr. Windberg to get closer to me, to leave Dubai. Even the father may have ulterior motives, like meeting with a new doctor to become the family's private physician. Who knows?"

"What will you do about the father?" Beau asked Jonas.

"I'm not sure," Jonas said. "It's deemed a diplomatic mission at the moment."

"Hardly," Jax said. "Not when he's played a major part in taking over that cruise liner."

"True, but we don't have any proof," Jonas argued. "He was never there, by your own accounts, and, as far as he's concerned, he'll probably say his head of security had gone off on his own rampage."

Jax nodded. "So you'll arrest him on suspicion of terrorist activities? Or are you letting him come in and leave again?"

"I highly doubt the little boy will leave anytime soon, will he?" he asked, turning toward Abby.

She shrugged. "I haven't a clue. I haven't seen his medical records. I haven't seen anything about him, no recent history at all."

"I do have something that was given to me about twenty minutes ago," Jax said. "I could forward it to your email."

"Good," she said. She finished her plate, stood, collected all their dishes, and put it on the trolley. "That might hold me for a little bit."

"We have dessert coming too," Jax said, "with a big pot of coffee."

At that, she nodded, cleared off her space, and got her laptop. He took the dishes to the door just in time to see the dessert and coffee tray coming. He exchanged the trolleys, brought the new one in, and served coffee. There were enough desserts for them to have several.

"What are you looking at?" Jonas asked.

"The boy's medical records," she said. "I'm trying to figure out the details of the blood disease and why he has it."

"Is there a why?" Jonas asked in interest.

"Sometimes," she said. "Not always. But I'm not seeing very much in the records here. I need X-rays. Blood work. Biopsy results. So far, nothing like that is here. His file should be thick with test results." She frowned and quietly asked, "Do we even know if the little boy is coming?"

Jax looked at her. "What do you mean?"

"Well, I need to see more obviously," she said, "because I have no medical confirmation of any blood disease."

At that, a dead silence hit the room.

CHAPTER 9

Abby wasn't even sure what to say about what she had seen, but obviously she didn't have everything. She didn't even have the most important data. "Somebody needs to get me an up-to-date medical file," she said crossly. "And I want the results where this cancer is supposed to be sitting and exactly what treatment he's already gone through."

"You're saying that all of our security for the hospital isn't even necessary?" asked Jonas.

"How do I know?" she said. "I'm only looking at the medical side of it." She closed her laptop and stood. "And obviously I'm not seeing much of the medical part either."

"Is it really missing that much information?"

She nodded. "And I'm not prepared to go through all his history from years ago if I don't have anything current." She was too tired to deal with any of this, even though eating had taken off the edge. Her phone also held a ton of messages from friends and colleagues, checking up on her. She wanted privacy, and she didn't want to deal with any of this anymore. She waved a hand at the men and said, "I'm heading to bed. Make your plans. At this rate, I'll need time to study Abdul's latest medical records, once they arrive—if they ever are produced—before I can even be effective. If I can do anything, treatments are not something we just whip out of our butts." She muted her angry tone but then said, "No,

I'm not pissed off at you guys. I'm pissed off at the circumstances."

She walked into her room and very carefully closed the door behind her. If anything, she just had to be alone for a few minutes. Since she'd first found Jax, she hadn't spent five minutes alone, except for her nap. He was either there with her, returning to her or dragging her behind him at all times. They'd been on the same ship together, had flow together, and were always sharing space, but never apart. Until tonight.

She walked over to the window, pulled up a chair, and sat down so she could just look out and be alone for a few minutes. To just *be* for a few minutes. What the hell was going on with Abdul's medical records? That bothered her more than a little. She didn't see any results from any blood test.

She didn't see anything.

Was the boy even sick? Had Dr. Windberg even treated him? Or was it all just a ploy to get her over there? In which case, how would she even know what she was supposed to be doing in England or what she was involved in or what scenario Dr. Windberg had created so the child's father believed the scumbag doctor?

And what massive long con had Dr. Windberg concocted this time? Did he not have any semblance of care anymore for the little boy? Or was he complicit, making the boy sick, so it looked like he needed more than the good doctor could provide?

Unfortunately she'd seen several similar cases. Usually the parents making their kids sick so the parents got more attention—a psychological disorder called Munchausen syndrome by proxy. It wouldn't be a first. But a doctor?

Even a bad doctor? Unfortunately cases like that could be found going back decades. But, as far as she could see, the child was just a means to an end. She had last seen Dr. Windberg at least five years ago, but the meeting was vivid in her mind. Mostly because she had just escaped his clutches and had crawled out the window and dropped almost two stories down to a hillside, hurting her ankle badly in the process.

But he had just laughed and said that she wouldn't get away forever and that, when she least expected it, she'd turn around, and he'd be right there, standing and waiting for her. And, in fact, that's exactly what had happened here.

She looked down at her hands, trembling even now. "Dear God," she whispered, "what on earth is Windberg up to?"

And how and why did it involve her? She did nothing more than be a student in the same classes as him. She'd been friendly and polite but never overly so. She couldn't afford to. She was so busy with med school and all her side jobs, trying to keep herself in food and with a roof over her head. She hadn't been one of the wealthy in the world. She hadn't had much choice.

But she'd done the hard work because the end result had been exactly what she had wanted. All she'd ever cared about was making it to med school and becoming the doctor she'd always dreamed about being. And, once there, she had no intention of just being a general practitioner. She'd gone into research, looking for cures and looking for stem-cell methodologies to improve. And so much was going on in the industry that the rapid-fire developments had almost left her in their wake.

And then she came up with this newer system on her

own. And that had been purely by accident, but, once it started to gel and take shape, it sped up the process tremendously, making stem-cell transplants so much easier with fewer rejections. Not all cancers responded to this treatment but some did and some did not. It's just odd that this doctor had followed her all this time and then had come up with a plausible scenario within her specialty for the little boy he was supposedly looking after.

In her heart of hearts, she knew that her greatest sorrow would be to find that this doctor had done something to hurt the child and that all those deaths on the cruise ship were meaningless in the wake of this man's obsession with her. She'd have done anything to turn time back and had him not killing those passengers, but she hadn't even known about it until the gunfire had swept through the place. And, even now, just the thought of seeing the doctor again made her physically ill. He'd been the stuff of nightmares. ... And she knew that the coming days would be the worst of her life.

It didn't matter how much Jax and Beau were there for her. They didn't fully understand what Dr. Windberg was like.

⚓

JAX WORRIED ABOUT her state of mind. Obviously she was tired, and her hunger had added to that, and maybe a good night's rest would help. But her stress was evident. He motioned Jonas to the now-empty seat and said, "Do you want to join us?"

Jonas nodded, sat down, and said, "I didn't mean to upset her."

"Something in the files upset her," Beau said.

"I think more than anything the whole scenario is upsetting," Jax said. "And, if something is missing in the file, she's got to be wondering what the doctor is up to."

"Sounds like he's a pretty shady character to begin with," Jonas said quietly. "He's got a history of stalking and obsessive behavior. And yet, he's been manipulating all this to bring her back into his sphere again."

"Which makes me worried about what his plan is at the hospital," Beau said.

"Exactly," Jonas said. "And I admit the hospital's not very impressed at being involved in this. They'll do what they can for the boy but …"

"Right."

They went over the security detail plan, with their orders to stay at the hotel and to not leave the vicinity in any way for the next thirty-six hours. Then they'd be met here Tuesday morning at eight by the MI6 security detail.

"Isn't that early for an afternoon appointment?" Beau asked.

"We want her at the hospital well before she'd be expected," Jonas explained.

Beau shrugged. "If I were Dr. Windberg, I'd already have this hospital under surveillance, and I'd already know that you were here in our hotel with us."

"Well, let's hope that this guy's more of a doctor and that his head of security is much less than intelligent."

"I think the head of security was intelligent enough," Jax said, recalling the look in the guy's eyes when he realized that he had lost the game. "I just wish I knew what the doctor was up to."

"The cruise ship was really a bizarre scenario," Beau said.

"They could have gotten on board as passengers, found out which room was hers, and taken her quietly off at the next port."

"I was thinking about that too," Jax said. "I think the head of security was used to engaging using more force than finesse."

"Which is why we really need to speak to the father," Jonas said. "He's the man behind all this. We can't have him thinking he can just take a cruise ship under his control and kill a few passengers in order to get what he wants."

"Have they entered the country yet?" Beau asked.

Jonas shook his head. "Not yet."

"You must have considered that they have methods of getting into the country without being noticed," Beau said.

"We've considered that," he said. "You know we can't watch all the shorelines. But the coast guards have been alerted. Everybody has received a bulletin saying that this family is trying to come in and that nobody is to stop them, yet we want to be notified immediately when they do."

"That's as good as it'll get," Jax said as he stood. "Are you coming back here tomorrow or the next day?"

Jonas shook his head. "I won't be coming back if I don't have to. You guys have things well under control. If you can keep her under wraps, then we're all good." On that note, he rose and walked out.

Jax sat here with half a piece of cake in front of him and a cup of tea. "I thought we ordered coffee," he asked, studying the pot.

"You might have, but, if you didn't stipulate that, then they brought tea. You are in England, after all," Beau said with a grin.

"What do you think was in that medical file that upset

her?"

"I think it's what *wasn't* in the file that upset her," he said calmly. "She can't take the kid's history in just an hour or even maybe an afternoon and sit down and have a consult. She needed to have the entire medical file."

"So he's keeping something from her is what you mean?" Jax nodded. "That would be in character."

Beau nodded. "Either that or they have no intention of letting her see the boy at all."

"Are you thinking that he wants her to fail?"

"Or potentially setting her up to fail. Although I'm surprised they haven't arrived already. Especially considering what they went through to get Abby here."

"They'll arrive soon enough," Jax said with a surety to his tone that he didn't really feel.

"Well, if they don't, it makes you wonder what they'll try next."

"Maybe give up the farce? If the father now knows the child's doctor is not reliable …"

Beau shook his head. "Not likely. I can't see these guys giving up. They might decide to take out a few more people just as a matter of form, but it'll be because they're pissed off."

"I hear you," Jax said. "We'll keep her locked up in the hotel all day tomorrow. So they better show up soon for the Tuesday meet."

"Good luck with that," Beau said. "I don't think she's anybody who locks up well."

CHAPTER 10

THE NEXT MORNING Abby was greeted by Jax. "What do you mean we can't go anywhere today? It's Monday morning. Early morning. The meet is not until Tuesday afternoon." She stared at Jax in astonishment. When he remained silent, she argued further, "We're in London. I have a few places I want to visit. Why can't I?"

"MI6's request," he stated firmly. "Sorry but no can do. Their security detail is arriving tomorrow at eight a.m. to assist us in escorting you to the hospital. In the meantime, you can't leave this hotel."

She sank into the chair closest to him and stared at him. "Seriously?"

"Seriously. Remember why we're here and the only reason we're here. We won't look at all the touristy hot spots or do some shopping," he snapped. "We're here until the family arrives, so we can get you safely to the hospital tomorrow, and so we can keep you safely there, and that's it."

She crossed her arms over her chest and then crossed her legs letting one swing in a snappy movement and glared at him. "That doesn't mean our visit has to be terrible. I haven't been on a holiday in years. That's likely why the attack on the cruise. It's the only time I've left my lab. And seriously the only time I've left the US. And Benjamin can't return there."

"Interesting theory," he said, "but you can make the best out of this quite nicely. Yet what you can't do is make this into something other than what it is."

"And what is it?"

"It's a hostage-taking scenario," he said, his tone cool but hard. "You set demands. They're meeting them. But, at the same time, you're forcing a lot of other people to dance to your tune to make this happen."

Immediately her arms fell away, and she stared at him in astonishment, then cried out, "Well, that's not what I meant to do."

"What you meant to do, I'm sure, was be a doctor treating a patient," he said. "But it doesn't matter at this point. It's all about where you're at now."

"That's terrible," she said, frowning. "I didn't want this to be a horrible and complicated scenario."

"Maybe," he said. "But the fact of the matter is that is exactly what has happened here. A lot of men, security and otherwise, are now on the lookout for these people."

She turned her gaze to the city all around them. She'd really been hoping that she could be a tourist for part of the day, to forget the cruise and the holiday that she no longer got to enjoy, and to forget about the upcoming meeting with the man of her nightmares, but instead, she would be locked up here or at the hospital, waiting on the child's arrival, with nothing better to do than surfing on the internet or further worrying. She got up, walked to the coffeepot, poured herself a cup, and took it to the window, where she leaned against the window frame and stared outside. "It seems strange to be a prisoner again."

"You're hardly a prisoner," he said.

"It's exactly what I am," she said. "But that's all right. I'll be an adult about it because you guys are still trying to help me. And that is much appreciated."

"We are," Beau said, coming out of his bedroom for the first time that morning.

She smiled up at him. "Don't you look bright and cheerful?"

"If I do, that's a mistake," he said. "I need at least three cups of coffee before I hit that level." He headed for the pot, poured the last of it, and immediately put on another one.

"And you're well-trained," she said. "That's always good to see."

He snorted. "Nothing well-trained about it. I just know my caffeine requirements, and nobody else will make it for me."

She chuckled. Jax stared at both of them and then buried his head in his laptop. She studied him, wondering why he didn't appear to like the banter between her and Beau. But, then again, if ever anybody would show an edge, it was him. Beau, with his size, was much more affable and friendly. She glanced around at the hotel room. "Are you guys staying here all day too then?"

Beau nodded. "That's the plan. Sleep a little, surf a little, eat a lot."

She burst out laughing. "Given your size, I'd imagine you do need to eat a lot."

He patted his tummy and said, "Dinner was a little skimpy last night."

"Good," she said. "Make sure you order some decent breakfast. But I'm hoping for lunch outside to find some fish and chips somewhere."

"The hotel will have it," Jax said.

"Yeah, but not the same thing as from a corner chip

vendor."

"We'll see," Beau said.

She sighed. "And that just sounds like a parent putting off a child who's been difficult. That's a half-baked promise that, if he eats his vegetables, he gets to go to the park in the afternoon." Beau looked at her in surprise. She shrugged. "Whatever." She walked back to where her laptop was and turned it on. "Maybe I'll get lucky today and find something interesting to watch on TV."

"And you have whatever you can surf on the web on your laptop," Beau said.

She nodded and brought up her emails. Seventeen downloaded. She groaned. "People need to understand that, if I don't get to have a life, they shouldn't be sending me all these emails."

"That's an odd way to look at it."

"Whatever," she said. "I just don't like answering emails."

"Why?"

"Lots of business to tend to," she said. "And I'm not at the office."

"Don't you have a business email?"

"Yes, but lots of people contact me privately," she said. "Although these look to be a couple updates from previous patients. This one's getting married, and I've been invited to the wedding. This guy was dying but is now doing fine, and his wife is pregnant again." She smiled and perked up. "These were actually good news." She quickly answered the ones that she could, parked one, deleted a couple, and then she got to the last one and said, "Oh no."

"What's *oh no*?"

She lifted her head from her laptop and said, "The asshole doctor. He just sent me an email. *Dearly beloved Abby, I'm looking forward to seeing you. I'm so grateful for your cooperation,*" she read out loud. "*See you soon.*"

"Seriously?" Jax asked. "So he reacts as if nothing is out of the ordinary about this request?"

"That would be him," she said. "He has no idea how to interact with people."

"Will you answer him?" Beau asked.

"Hell no," she said. "I don't even know how he got my personal email address." She quickly closed her laptop, more disturbed than she could say. Then she hopped up and walked over to the coffee. She poured a cup fresh from the pot that Beau had made and said, "Just even reading his words sends shivers down my spine."

"Just how bad is this guy?" Beau asked.

She shrugged, not wanting to discuss Windberg at all. Yet she knew she should give these guys more details so they would have a more complete picture to work with. "He's beyond scummy. And I always figured that he was the kind who would keep somebody chained up downstairs in their basement and feed them only to keep them alive long enough to abuse them for years on end—and yet, have it all twisted around in his head that he was saving them for something better." Her tone conveyed such a sense of disgust that she winced. "Look. Maybe he's changed. Maybe I'm just being too hard on him." Both men shot her a hard look. She shrugged and nodded. "No, I know I'm not."

"It's hard to imagine what he's thinking," Jax said. "But, as you know, he stalked you. He made disturbing phone calls and sent you voicemail messages and texts. He followed you, and he attacked you. This doesn't seem like the same efforts on his part. Almost like a very different man."

"No," she said. "It's bigger, much bigger. He's always been the king of the long con. He used to get the profs wrapped around his fingers, and then, by the time they figured out what he was up to, the class was over. Most of them would just shake their heads, try to figure out what had happened, but then moved on. But for those of us students who were forced to live with him and his actions, we knew there was no moving on. And you just avoided him like the plague."

"So you can see him doing something like this?"

"I think the cruise was over-the-top," she said. "And I highly doubt that was solely his work. I think that was more of the father's work. If you're asking if Windberg would have minded if people died fulfilling his wishes, the answer is hell no. He would have ordered the attacks himself if he thought it would have gotten him what he wanted."

"I don't like this guy at all," Beau said.

"Well, stand in line," Jax said, "because you don't get to hit him until I have first."

"That's just because you know I hit harder than you," Beau said complacently.

Jax raised his gaze, narrowed it at Beau, and snorted. "You wish."

The two men fell back to verbally wrangling again. Abby sighed, sat down, and said, "Do we get food? I'm hungry."

Beau patted her gently on the shoulder. "See? A woman after my own heart."

"Can we go to the hotel restaurant at least?"

Jax nodded. "Jonas didn't say, *sequestered in our hotel rooms*. He said, *sequestered in the hotel*."

"Perfect," she said. "Let's go down, hit the tourist shop, go to the cafeteria or whatever they have, and have a proper

English breakfast."

"I'm not eating a proper English breakfast," Beau said. "I want real food."

She glanced at him in surprise. "You mean, you want American food," she corrected.

"Whatever," he said. "I want meat, meat, and more meat."

At that, she laughed and started to close the laptop in front of Jax. "Are you coming?"

He nodded. "Hold on. Let me finish."

"Sure, as long as you tell me what you're doing," she said with a smile.

"I'm redoing our route to and from the hospital with a couple alternatives in case we run into trouble."

"In the hospital or out of the hospital?" she asked.

"Both," he said. "I've got the blueprints memorized just in case."

She stopped, looked at him, and said, "Just in case what?"

"Just in case they decide to take the hospital hostage the same as they did the cruise ship."

⚓

FROM THE PALING of her skin, it was obvious that Abby hadn't considered such a scenario.

"I hope you're wrong," she said in a hoarse whisper. "Jesus, I hope you're wrong."

"It's a much more vulnerable place to take," Jax said. "If you think about it, a lot of people will be caught up in this mess too. If the good doctor tries something like that, we're all in deep trouble."

She pinched the bridge of her nose and said, "I'm sorry. I was only thinking of the little boy."

"I know you were," he said. "And I appreciate that, but we can't dismiss that the father may only understand brutish methods, and that's the same methods they will use at the hospital."

"Oh, boy," she said. "Then all I'm doing is putting hundreds more people at risk."

He nodded. "Exactly. Much better to have gone to Dubai."

"And something about that felt *so* wrong," she whispered. "I just knew I wasn't coming back alive."

"Maybe," he said, "but we also must consider that maybe it would leave everybody else alive."

She glared at him. "We're back to that me instead of twenty-five hundred, right? Well, I was agreeable then, so I can hardly argue now."

"Well, we must consider something," he said. "Just think about it."

She would, but it wasn't appealing. "So what am I supposed to do? I don't want anybody at the hospital put at risk."

He laughed. "Too late. They already are."

"Argh," she said. "Can we count on MI6 for security in this case?"

"Well, we hope so," Beau said. "But obviously we'll do a bit more work on that to make sure that we aren't relying only on them. Because, as soon as you do that, all hell breaks loose."

"True enough," she said. "Let's go eat, and then we can come back and maybe think about this some more."

Jax laughed. "It's all we'll be thinking about for the next

twenty-four hours and beyond. That's just what it is."

"Got it," she said. "But still, I want to make sure that we're as safe as we can be and that everybody in that hospital is as safe as can be. I can say it until I'm blue in the face. I'm sorry. I just didn't know what else to do."

"And you played your hand, and it's happening," he said. "Now we make sure that the hand that you end up with is one that we can work with."

She nodded slowly. "It sucks though."

"Oh, it does," he said. "It sucks big time. But it doesn't change anything, does it?"

"No," she whispered, "it doesn't."

On that note, she walked out the door, and Beau stuck to her like glue. Jax remained behind, wanting to look at his phone and see the last text that had come in. Something was definitely happening here that would not be too easy to sort out while she was around.

He checked his phone to find Jonas's text, telling Jax that father, son, and entourage, nine in all, had arrived. Jax winced at that. He quickly sent back a text message, asking who were all in the entourage. The response, when it came, was to be expected. Some were obvious mentions: security, the head of security, and the doctor. One female, presumably the mother, and then four other men. Likely part of his security detail. Something that they would all keep in mind. He raced after Beau, catching them just as they went into the restaurant. Beau lifted an inquiring eyebrow. Jax nodded and said, "The family has arrived."

She sucked in her breath.

He caught the sound, gripped her hand in his, and said, "Chess pieces. Remember? They're all coming into play now."

She nodded. "I did tell you that I was lousy at the game, right?"

He chuckled. "You didn't need to tell us that. We already knew."

She snorted. "I'm not that bad."

"Glad to hear that," he said, "because we have an awful lot of stuff to keep track of right now. That's very important."

"I know," she said quietly. "It's all about tomorrow."

CHAPTER 11

WHEN THE NEXT day finally dawned, Abby was grateful to have something to do. Sitting on edge the whole day yesterday, waiting for something to happen and yet knowing they couldn't do anything while in this waiting phase, drove her crazy. She'd woken a couple times in the night but finally made it through to a truly reasonable hour of the morning. Now she had showered and sat in the living room with her first cup of coffee.

The men were on their phones. Always. She just shook her head, wondering why she still hadn't received anything on the child's file and worried that she already knew the answer. As they walked over to join her in the living area, she said, "What's the chance of being waylaid on the way to the hospital?"

"A little too big," he said. "It's something we've considered."

She nodded. "Good."

"Is that what you think will happen?" Beau asked as he sat down.

"Not really." She shrugged. "Yet it's something I have to consider."

"We're planning for it," he said. "So not to worry."

At the restaurant, she, Beau, and Jax sat down and ordered breakfast. Jax was a little on edge, his gaze studying the area. He contacted Jonas to let him know they were on the move.

"Make sure you keep all your sensors live," Jonas said.

"We still have them," Jax said. "Are we all showing up online?"

"Yes," Jonas said. "All three of you are tagged, bagged, and ready to go."

"Don't put it that way," Jax said, "but, if you have to, perfect," he said. With that, he put the phone down beside them and looked at Abby and smiled. "Sorry for using my phone at the table."

She rolled her eyes. "Like that's the biggest problem facing me right now."

"Well, you never know," he said. "I don't mean to be rude."

She gripped his fingers and smiled. "If you're weren't, I would think you were sick."

Beau chuckled at that.

Jax just rolled his eyes at her, and, when the waitress came, they quickly ordered, and the food was delivered promptly. He looked down at it, but all his senses were alive. He wasn't exactly sure what was bunching up the hairs in the back of his neck, so he looked at Beau, and there he met his partner's gaze.

Beau nodded, his face staring past Jax's head. "We've got company."

"But is it company we want to see?" Jax asked nonchalantly as he picked up a piece of toast, his gaze going to the picture behind Beau's head, checking the reflection there, seeing if he could get something off the glass. But it was a shitty reflection. He waited until their *company* walked past, following a waitress to get to a table. Jax looked up, frowned, and said, "Interesting. They brought the fight to us."

Abby leaned forward and whispered, "What?"

He tilted his head toward the table where two men just sat down. She turned her head, caught sight of the head of security they'd seen on the cruise liner, and immediately put down her knife and fork. She stared at Jax and Beau. "I'm not feeling very hungry all of a sudden."

"Doesn't matter," Jax said. "You need to eat. For fuel, just in case you need to run."

She glared at him, stared at the food, and then systematically ate. He doubted that she enjoyed any bite of it, but there was no doubt it was an effective manner. And when she laid down her fork ten minutes later, she said, "Can we leave now?"

"Yes," he said. "So now we can head home or back up to our room, and our company won't care. Because they've already confirmed that we're here. Getting a lock on us here, they can keep track of us."

"Speaking of tracking," she said.

"Yes, we're being tracked by a lot of people right now. And quite possibly by them too."

Back up in her room, the reality of what she was doing just set in. Somehow she'd blocked out all thoughts of this doctor and the pain that he'd caused her—well, most of them. But there was no more ignoring what was happening. Especially not when it was directly in front of her now. There was no way out of this. There was no way to do anything but get through this mess. And, if she could at least just get through it, then she could put it behind her.

She was worrying more about the sick boy now. Determining a condition, establishing a treatment plan, and getting it started couldn't be done in an hour. It wouldn't be a simple case of just doing a couple tests to see what was wrong.

And still, in the back of her mind, she didn't think the boy's supposed illness had anything to do with a disease. It all had to do with Benjamin Windberg. Benjamin, the man she'd hated for years. The man who still terrified her. And yet, she wondered at his campaign of fear. It was so effective that, back then, she hadn't slept well for days or weeks after his attack. Only after she heard that he'd finally left the country had she calmed down enough to put it behind her. Now years later, Benjamin's game of fear reared its ugly head again.

She sat down, looking at her hands. Her fingers still shook. She also knew her cheeks had to be pale because everything inside her had a clamminess to it. She didn't know how to deal with this. It had been years since she'd seen him. Years during which she'd worked hard and fought long to put it behind her. Or at least seemingly did.

And, just like that, knowing that she could possibly see him again today, even seeing the head of security, the man who had been responsible for the carnage on the cruise ship, to know that both of those men were walking free and clear, her stomach heaved. She raced to the toilet and lost her breakfast.

In the deep recesses of her mind, she knew Benjamin would be after her again. She knew that his ego wouldn't allow him to not try again. He had to win. Failure was a huge blow to his ego—his lying smooth-talking way and just that sliminess to him scared the crap out of her.

"You're not alone, you know," Jax said as he crouched down beside her. He picked up one of her hands that had been lying in her lap and rubbed her fingers, obviously picking up on the fact that they were chilled, and so was she.

She looked at him but couldn't muster a smile. "I know I'm not alone," she said, "but you don't understand who this man is."

"Maybe you should tell us more," Beau said, standing in the doorway to her bathroom.

She shrugged. "There's not much I can tell you. Just that he has this incredible way of making everybody afraid of him. I was just thinking about the campaign of fear he ran against me and how all it took was the sound of his voice to send me into absolute shock." She paused, then said, "I'm terrified of meeting him today. And I know that doesn't say much about me being strong, and I'm sorry because I would like to be better than this …"

"Stop right there," Jax said. "You are doing incredibly well. Don't ever let yourself think otherwise. I get that you think this is a horrible scenario, where you're supposed to stand up to this and face it and then toss it off with a semblance of nonchalance. That's how the movie-goers would have you act. But it's not that way. Life is not that easy. It's not that simple. This man did run a campaign of fear against you, and I really like that terminology, by the way. That's exactly what he did. It was all about power. It was all about abuse. It was always about keeping you terrified. And, because he had the power to do so, he kept pushing it and pushing it. You'd have given him anything to have him out of your life."

She nodded. "I would have," she whispered. "I still would."

He immediately squeezed her fingers. "And that's what I mean. Benjamin being here is not the end of the world. We are both here for you. Benjamin won't get a hold of you."

She gave a half snort of laughter. "He's gone to a lot of trouble to get his hands on me again. The chances of him doing it again are pretty darn good."

Beau asked, "Any idea what he might have up his sleeve?"

She looked at Beau and answered his question. "Not really. My mind keeps going to the worst scenarios possible. And it would require assistance from other men to make any of those scenarios happen. But he obviously has some people around, willing to help him get what he wants."

"What scenarios?"

She looked at Jax. "I keep thinking he'll likely knock me out or hit me with a pressure syringe that knocks me cold, and then I get spirited away to a private jet back to Dubai."

"Dubai isn't exactly a lawless land though," Beau said. "Obviously we don't want that happening, but something about Dubai terrifies you even more."

"Sure," she said. "I could disappear there, and nobody would be the wiser. I could end up in a sheikh's harem out in the middle of nowhere, and nobody would ever find me again."

"Except for us," Jax said with such a note of certainty that she stared at him in surprise.

"What will you do against all that Iraqi military manpower?" she asked.

He gave a gurgle of laughter. "What we've always done against military manpower. Be sneakier, faster, and better. We would bring you home. I promise you."

She looked at him, slowly studying the look in his eyes, and then smiled. "I know you believe that."

He shook his head. "It doesn't matter what I believe. It matters what you believe because, when you walk in that hospital, if you're looking over your shoulder every step of the way, you can't do your job. You can't focus on what you do, and you'll be getting in our way. We need to focus on our job, and you need to focus on your job. But, in order for that to work properly, you must trust us."

She took a deep but shaky breath. "You're asking for a lot."

"Exactly," Beau said cheerfully. "And, speaking of which, it's almost time to go."

Her breath was once again shaky. She nodded and said, "Already?"

"Yep. Time to sneak you out of here."

Her eyebrows shot up. "I thought the whole point was how they already know where we are?"

"Sure, they know that we're here. You can bet that they know that we're in this room in this hotel, but that doesn't mean that they get to know when or how we move."

"So we're not staying here? We'll stay at some other secret place after the hospital?"

"In case you didn't notice, your luggage has already been moved."

At that, she looked around, and her jaw dropped. "I didn't," she said. "Wow, am I completely out of it. Somebody took my luggage, and I didn't even see."

"It was moved while we were downstairs," Beau said. "We know we're being watched. So it's more of a case of making sure that you're moved as needed under the guise of secrecy."

"Well, cameras are up here," she said. "And just how will you stop that?"

At that, Jax's watch beeped. He stood, helped her to her feet, and said, "That signal tells us the cameras are off. Let's go." And she was quickly led out the door, across the hall to the set of stairs, and then moved two flights down. He sent a beep back on his watch.

She looked at him. "Was that the signal to say that we'd moved?"

He nodded.

⚓

BY THE TIME they had left the hotel, surrounded by MI6 men, out the rear door in the parking garage and into a vehicle heading toward the hospital, she had reverted to *Abby the doctor under extreme duress.* Jax knew that she felt she was doing the right thing, and likely she was, as far as her code of morals and ethics went. But most of the world didn't operate on the same scale of morality that she did. Which was too bad, because then a lot of people didn't understand her reactions to everything going on.

They were led into a hospital door, through the morgue area. And then back up through service elevators to the floor that they needed. With Jax and Beau at her side, they finally walked into a small waiting room. There was a woman and a small boy.

Jax was not surprised that they were here early. As Jax scanned the room, he first saw the head of security eating breakfast across from him.

The woman looked up, and everybody could see the worry in her eyes, but, more than that, the uncertainty too as she shuffled in place, dressed in a dark burka, and kept pushing her sleeve up and then pulling it back down again. She was almost as uncomfortable as Abby was. Abby reached out and introduced herself, shaking the woman's hand.

The woman nodded gratefully. "My son," she whispered, "can you help my son?"

Abby looked at him and said, "I don't have his full medical file. Do you?"

The woman glanced around, up in the corners, as if looking for a camera. And then she quickly handed over a small USB key. Abby turned it around in her fingers for a moment and said to Beau, "I need my laptop."

Beau disappeared.

Jax asked the woman, "Where is your husband?"

"With his security team."

"Do you know where exactly?"

The scared woman shook her head. "No, but he is inside the hospital somewhere, nearby, in case he is needed."

In the meantime, in a small private room, Abby did a full physical exam, checking the little boy's chest, lungs, eyes, throat, and heart. It was obvious that the child was somewhere around four or maybe five years old, but he didn't speak English, adding a language barrier to the interview. Finally, when she was done, Beau returned with her laptop. She opened it up, put the key in, and transferred the information. Then she sat here for a few minutes, studying the results. "Do you know what treatments have been done?"

The woman took a deep breath and shook her head. "My husband doesn't let me see such things."

"Interesting," she said.

Jax watched the look on Abby's face as he perused everything going on. He could tell from the stillness in her face that she didn't understand what she saw. She opened up several more files and then looked at the mother and said, "I need to pull some blood and run some more tests."

The woman nodded immediately. "But I don't know

what else you could possibly test for. He's very ill."

"And the doctor told you it was cancer?"

The mother nodded.

"I don't see any scans. I don't see any biopsy reports," Abby asked. "Do you know what kind of cancer?"

"Stomach cancer," the mother said. And then she stopped, frowned, and said, "I think, but I'm not sure."

"Well, let me draw some blood," Abby said. She looked at Beau. "I need the equipment to pull some or a nurse to pull some blood."

The mother shook her head. "You must do it."

"Why is that?"

"My husband says so. Nobody else must touch his son."

She nodded, looked at Beau, and said, "Tell one of the nurses I need a kit."

He returned a moment later with a blue plastic kit, several vials and syringes and plastic containers. He handed it over and said, "I didn't know how much you needed."

"This will be fine," she said. She quickly took a sample of blood, filling one and a half vials, and then wrote up a lab order.

And from what Jax could see, she was asking for extensive testing from all the check marks he saw her making.

Then, Abby turned, halted, added one more note at the top: Rush on Arsenic Presence.

Jax frowned at her note.

"I don't need to tell you," she said to Beau as she handed everything back to him, "but this takes top priority, as in everybody drops everything now. And either you or one of the MI6 security team must stay with the sample and the tester at all times."

"We're on it," he said, and he walked out again.

At that, the mother seemed to relax slightly.

As soon as Abby had downloaded all the material, she ejected the USB key and handed it back. The key disappeared into the folds of the mother's burka without any sign of it ever having been here.

Jax had to wonder if the mother had taken that and had handed it over without the father's permission.

"What I still don't have are the files from Abdul's current doctor. With his notations, suppositions, and analyses," she said, looking at the mother. "Do you have any of that?"

The mother shook her head. "He doesn't tell me. My husband does not tell me."

"So you don't have it, or you don't know about it, or the doctor won't tell you?"

"The doctor does not tell me."

"Okay," she said. She walked over to the little boy and smiled down at him.

The child did look pretty sickly, as far as Jax was concerned, and looked like he'd lost some hair. His skin was pale too. Abby checked his eyes over again a second time and then slowly palpitated his stomach. Even Jax could tell she didn't find anything. The little boy made no cry of pain and had no distress of any kind. He just lay here, almost comatose.

Abby looked back at the mother and asked, "How long has he been so lethargic?"

The mother's shoulders shook. "Weeks now," she whispered brokenly. "Every day, it gets worse."

"Right," she said. "What I don't know is whether we'll be in time to save him."

At that, the mother started to cry.

Jax spoke up, "Do you know what's wrong with him?"

"Not for sure until the testing comes back," she said. "But I think he's been poisoned." The mother shrieked. Immediately the little boy rolled over and reached out a hand, wanting his mother.

Abby said to the mother, "Calm down, please. We don't want anything to upset him."

Sniffing noisily, the woman tried hard to stop her tears, and Abby went back to study the boy's fingernails and his hair and his lips. "I can start treatment right away, but I need the results back to make sure that we're not going down the wrong pathway."

"What kind of a pathway?" Jax asked.

She tilted her head toward the mother so that Jax was supposed to get a message of some kind. He realized that Abby didn't want the mother to know. He didn't understand that because it was likely already well past the point of keeping it from her. "Is there an antidote?"

"Not if too much has been given for too long," she said. "It'll be touch-and-go. He's showing pretty severe signs."

"But the other doctor, wouldn't he have known?"

At that, the mother looked at her and said, "Yes, would he not have known?"

She hesitated. "It's not something that presents itself very often," she said slowly. "It's honestly not even my expertise. But I have seen one other case like this."

Jax stood closer and asked, "What kind of poison?"

She looked at him and whispered, "Arsenic."

CHAPTER 12

ABBY HOPED SHE was wrong, but the child was presenting with those symptoms. She pulled out her phone and contacted a physician she knew. Quickly she explained what she had found and that she was waiting on the blood work to come back.

"You should have that within four hours," he said. "Depending on how severe it is …"

"I know, but you have no idea how much trauma other people have been through because of this. If there's anything we can do to help this little boy …"

"There's a couple really radical treatments we could try," he said. "I am in London."

She straightened and smiled. "Can I get you over here then, please?"

"It's not like I have any rights to work there," he warned.

"I can clear that instantly. Anything to save this little guy."

"I'll be about thirty minutes."

She turned back to Jax and said, "I need you to get him cleared to be here."

His eyebrows shot up.

She shook her head. "He's an American doctor with no rights to work here, but he does have colleagues here. He's at a workshop. I need him here because he's the one who could treat this poisoning if anything might work here. He said there's only a couple radical options." She turned to look back at the mother, who now sobbed silently in place, then turned to Jax. "I need the blood work back immediately too."

He nodded, opened the door, and there was Beau, standing outside. They spoke quickly, and then Jax shut the door and sat back down again. She frowned at him. He shrugged and said, "I'm not leaving your side."

She glanced at him and then gave him a small smile. "Thanks."

"You realize that, regardless of what happens, we must find out who has been poisoning him?"

She nodded. She turned back to the mother and said, "We need to talk."

It was all the mother could do to contain her emotions, but eventually she calmed down enough that, with a box of tissues in her hand, she could speak.

"Do you know anybody who would have been poisoning your little boy?" She named off a bunch of foods where the arsenic came naturally and said, "It's also found in various medications. Also in a lot of poisons, like to use in the garden or for eliminating nuisance rodents, such as rat poison," she said.

The mother just stared at her.

"Do you know if Abdul would have come into contact with any of that?"

The woman shook her head.

"And what about in the boy's food? Who arranges his food?"

"I do," she says. "We have a cook as well, but I supervise all his food."

"Why?" Jax asked.

She turned to look at him. "Nahim has only one son and five daughters. He has wanted a son for a very long time. He makes sure that his son is okay."

"And does he have very many enemies?" Jax asked.

She just stared at him in growing horror. "Yes, yes," she said. "My husband does. But that's why I prepare his son's food. To make sure that nothing happens."

"And yet, you said this has been going on for a couple months?"

"He started getting sick over three months ago," she said.

"And yet, the doctor said it's cancer?"

"Yes, he's been vomiting lots, and he can't keep food down."

"And do you trust the cook who's been looking after him?"

A small smile crossed the woman's face. "Yes, it's my mother."

Abby thought it was pretty unlikely that a grandmother would do anything to hurt the obviously well-loved grandson. She nodded. "Okay, that makes sense." She tossed a glance at Jax. They both knew it would be Benjamin, who she hated so much. Somehow he gave the little boy just enough arsenic to keep him sick and to ensure Benjamin's services were needed. But, over time, it had taken its toll on the little boy. "How long has the doctor worked for you?"

"He worked for others in the family," she said, "but he's only been with us for a few months."

"And did you bring him on because your son got sick?"

"Abdul got sick first, and then we brought the doctor to him."

Abby sat down, stumped. "Interesting," she said.

"We would have done anything," the woman murmured, tears collecting again in her eyes. "Anything."

Abby nodded. "But you should also look after the baby you're carrying," she said gently.

The woman's hands immediately went to her belly. "Am I?"

Abby's eyebrows rose. "Are you not?"

She shrugged. "I've been so worried about Abdul that I haven't had any time to even think about it."

Abby studied her. "I would have said at least thirteen or maybe fourteen weeks along."

The woman nodded. "But that's how long it's been since Abdul got sick. He's been on my mind all the time."

Abby nodded, got up, went to the door, and spoke to Beau, asking him for a pregnancy kit. His eyebrows shot up. She shrugged and closed the door in his face. When he came back a few minutes later, she handed it to the woman and said, "Go to the bathroom and do this test."

The woman hesitated, but Abby said, "Go. We need all the information that we can gather."

The woman disappeared into the bathroom, leaving Abby standing beside Abdul. As soon as the door closed, Jax hopped to his feet and motioned Abby closer, then whispered, "What does Abdul's mother have to do with this?"

"Nothing maybe," she said. "But we must make sure that, if she is pregnant, the father knows, in case she gets punished for not looking after Abdul properly." When Jax sucked in his breath, she nodded. "There's a reason why she's been the one preparing Abdul's food. If somebody else has slipped Abdul something, the mother gets blamed. If she's pregnant, it might save her life."

"Jesus," Jax said, standing at her side, reaching up a hand to gently stroke her back. "How are you doing?"

She shrugged. "Every time I hear something, I think it's Benjamin coming," she said. "As far as I'm concerned, he poisoned this little boy. And somehow we must find out how he did it and stop him from doing it again."

"What do you want me to do?"

"Find out who else in the family Benjamin worked for and ask them, did anybody else suffer, get sick, or die while he was there?"

Just then the bathroom door opened, and Abdul's mother stepped out. The look on her face was both joy and shock. She held out the pregnancy test. "It's positive."

"Good," Abby said with a big smile. "Congratulations."

The woman sank down beside Abdul. Yet she hadn't smiled once.

"Is there any reason your husband won't be happy to hear this?" Jax asked.

The woman looked at him in surprise, not understanding the question.

Abby gently questioned her. "Jax wants to make sure that Abdul's father is the father of this child."

Immediately the woman nodded. "I would not dare," she said. "He'll be very happy."

"Good," Jax said, subsiding into his chair.

While they waited for the blood tests to come back, and she knew that the lab would do everything they could to make it happen as fast as possible, doing the arsenic test first and foremost. She didn't like anything about the condition of the boy, but she also needed Danny to get here fast. When a bunch of noise sounded in the adjoining waiting room, Jax hopped to his feet and went to the door right when Beau knocked. Jax opened it, and another man stepped forward.

The man walked over to Abby and gave her a big hug. "Damn, it's good to see you," he cried out.

She smiled, kissed him on the cheek, and said, "You too. But this is our focus right now."

He nodded, his gaze already on the little boy on the examination table. Then he walked forward, his frown already taking over. He looked at her and said, "Is he your patient?"

"He's just come from Dubai," she said, trying not to explain too much. "But I'm right, aren't I?"

"You are. We'll do a couple biopsies to see how far along it is and start blood transfusion treatments immediately. We can work on setting this up right away."

And as soon as he said that, the mother jumped out and reached out for Abby's hand. "My husband said only you."

"But your husband didn't know your son was being slowly murdered by poison," Abby said carefully. "Danny here, he's the best there is for this."

The woman looked at Danny, her eyes already filled with dread. "Can you help him?"

He smiled at her and said, "I don't know if we can save him, but I'll do my best." He looked at Abby. "Do you want to stay here or come with me?"

She smiled and said, "I must stay with Abdul."

"And your guard?"

"He—"

"—goes where she goes," Jax interrupted.

Danny nodded. "In that case, let's go for a hell of a ride."

JAX WAS AMAZED at the efficiency of the two doctors as they worked on the boy. As soon as they got the confirmed diagnosis of arsenic poisoning, they already had everything ready and went into action. Treatments were started; IV drips were set up; and biopsies were taken. Stem cells were next. Jax looked at Danny and said, "Do you know for sure how bad it is?"

"No," he said. "And the thing is, with a child, there is no bottom line. They have an incredible ability to heal. This little guy's had a hard time, but then the travel would have added to that too. It won't be a fast or easy solution, so it'll take a few days before we see if anything's improving." He looked at Jax and asked, "Can you do anything about the paperwork?"

"It's already in progress," Jax said. "Nobody here will argue."

"Well, that's a first," Danny said. "Most of the time, there's nothing but arguments."

"Entirely different scenario right now," Jax said.

"I'd love to hear the why of it."

"It'll make you sick to your stomach," Jax said. "And we really don't want the word getting out right now, so we appreciate everything you're doing without asking any questions."

Danny snorted. "All you military guys are the same."

"How do you know he's military?" Abby asked.

He glanced at her sideways. "Seriously?"

She nodded.

"You don't need a buzz cut to see that military bearing in his shoulders, that *take a step out of line and I'll kill you* look in his eye or the way he follows you like a hawk. You are his mission right now," Danny said with a big grin. "I just wonder if you're his mission at nighttime too."

She smacked him on the shoulder for his teasing.

But Jax wondered that too. No doubt she was his mission. No doubt that he had gotten closer to his mission than he should have. And, not for the first time, he thought about all the things about her that he really liked. He really liked a lot of other women too, but the difference here was that undefinable spark between them. That connection. He could sit down and talk with twenty different women he respected. They could all be gorgeous bombshells. But, if they didn't have that something, that special zing that went off whenever he touched her, then it was a completely different ball game. And with Abby, there was definitely that zing. And he was pretty damn happy about it himself.

Just then he caught Danny glancing at him with an appraising look in his eye.

Jax raised an eyebrow and asked, "Problem?"

"Nope." Danny shook his head. "Just that you're an interesting choice for her. ... My husband, Ronald, is very different."

Jax smiled and nodded. "I look forward to meeting him. It can't be easy to be partnered with a doctor."

"It's even worse because," Danny said, "Ronald is a musician. Lives in his own world. I don't think he knows when I'm gone half the time."

"Oh, yes, he does," Abby said, laughing. "I think his music helps him deal with missing you."

The conversation rolled on as the day passed in a blur of activity around the little boy. They ran more tests than Jax ever thought was even possible. They had specialists in and out, and, by the end of the normal workday, the little boy looked even more exhausted. They put him in a private room under a security guard with his mom at his side. And finally Abby walked over to Jax and asked, "Can we get some food?"

"We can," he said, "but it'll be brought in. None of us are leaving the hospital until this is over with."

She stared at him and then slowly nodded. "I'll be so glad to have this completely over."

He gave a small smile, not promising anything, and asked, "Any sign of your doctor?"

She shook her head. "No, but I'm sure he's here somewhere."

He nodded. "I'm sure he is too. Have you asked the mother?"

"No, she appears to be stressed enough," Abby said gently. "I didn't want to add to it."

"And maybe it would make her feel better to know that her son's doctor was here and cared enough to look after Abdul."

"Maybe," she said. "But a part of me doesn't think so. I can imagine that it's beyond stressful for her. And maybe with Windberg being another male, that doesn't help at all."

Jax winced at that. He couldn't imagine just what the mother's life was like if she was so under her husband's thumb as she made it out to be. And he could well believe her words because it wasn't an easy thing to deal with in Iraq. Dubai was very progressive compared to a lot of areas, but that didn't mean that her particular family scenario was.

"We'll find a place for you to rest and to get some food," he said. Then he hesitated, not sure how to tell her.

She looked up at him in surprise. "What's the deal?"

"I'm not sure it's safe to let Danny leave."

Her mouth circled into an *O* as she understood. "Well,

that's not good."

"I know. I was trying to figure out what to do about it."

"He won't take it kindly if we keep him as a prisoner. He's here as a favor."

"I know that," he said.

"Yes, so why would they hurt Danny?"

"Maybe," Jax spoke in a very low voice, "to keep you in line."

She winced. "These guys are really assholes, aren't they?"

"I don't know for sure," he said. "All we can do is presume, from what we've seen so far, and having done what they did on the cruise, I can't imagine that they'll care a whole lot about keeping Danny alive."

"No," she said softly. "They'll do everything they can to get their wishes met. And Danny is doing everything he can to save the boy." But she paled at the thought. "I couldn't live with myself if anything happened to him."

"I know," he said. "And obviously we'll do everything we can to keep him safe. I just don't know what that'll look like."

"Right," she said.

Just then came a knock on the door. She looked at Jax, and he motioned for her to back away from the entrance as two men stepped in. One of them, she recognized. It was the head of security from the cruise ship. She immediately pointed a finger at him. "You," she snapped. "What are you doing here?"

He stiffened, glared at her, and said, "I wouldn't be here at all if it wasn't for you."

"You're right," she agreed. "And you're welcome. You're only alive because of me."

He didn't like her saying that.

Jax immediately put up his hand and motioned her to calm down. He looked at the other man with the security guard and assessed him carefully, then realized this was probably Nahim. Right behind him, all he could see was an empty room. "Where is the guard?" he asked.

The head of security shrugged. "I don't know," he said. "It has nothing to do with us."

"Really?" she cried out. "Have you done anything to Beau?"

"I'm here," Beau said, stepping into her line of sight.

Jax looked at him and studied his face, but nothing untoward about his positioning said he was being held prisoner on the other side. Jax nodded toward the two newcomers and asked Beau, "You let them in?"

Beau said, "The father, yes. The security guard is staying here with me."

"No," the father said. "I don't go anywhere without my guard."

"Maybe," Jax said calmly. "But, if you want to see your son, you leave your killer soldier behind."

The father glared at him. But then Nahim heard a voice in the distant background.

"Papa?"

Jax watched the emotions work on the father's face, and then Jax stepped aside to let Nahim in. As soon as the security man stepped forward, Jax placed a hand against his chest and said, "Don't push it."

He glared at him. "I'm here to look after the boy. Do you really think I'll do anything to hurt him at this point?"

"I'm not sure," Jax said, "because the bottom line is, somebody has already hurt him deliberately."

The security guard looked at him in horror. "What are

you talking about?"

But Jax wouldn't elaborate. It wasn't the time or the place. "When we have all the answers, we'll tell you," he said. "In the meantime, we must ensure that our people are protected and that you don't get a chance to kill any more people."

The head of security nodded stiffly, but he added, "Like you, I'm only following orders."

"And we'll take that into account," Jax said. "But sometimes people enjoy their work a little too much." He referred to the killings on the cruise ship.

The other man just shrugged. "By any means possible. Like you haven't done whatever you needed to do to get the job done," he snapped.

"I have," Jax said, "but taking a life to make a point is not a method I agree with."

"Maybe not but we didn't all have choices."

Jax laughed at that. "If there's one thing you do understand, it's choice. We all had a lot of choices when it came to this."

He heard a gentle cry behind him. He turned to see the wife, held in her husband's arms. Jax was glad to see that. He wasn't sure at all if this was a happy family scenario or if she had been more of a prisoner herself. With Beau still standing in the doorway, Jax watched and waited at the tearful reunion between them all. When he looked back, he saw the head of security's eyes overcome by emotion too.

He studied them for a long moment. "You care, don't you?"

"He is my brother," he said. "And his son is my family."

"Maybe," Jax said. "But a lot of people have been killed for just that family relationship."

"Yes, quite true. But that is our way."

"It may be your way, but you killed a lot of other people's brothers and sons with your casual disregard for human life."

"Again, it is our way."

Not an answer that Jax wanted to hear, but he understood. It was a terrible thing. These guys were hardly at war with Abby, but they wanted Jax to believe it was that. And maybe, if he lived in their country and dealt with the lifestyle that they lived, maybe he'd see it that way too. He didn't know. It just seemed so wrong on so many levels.

The mother turned around and said to the security guard, "Thank you for looking after my son."

Jax heard Abby snort, and he realized there would likely be trouble. He quickly shoved the security guard outside and told Beau, "Keep him there." And then he shut the door quickly.

"Thank you for looking at my son today," the father said to Abby, like it pained him to do so.

Jax turned to face Abby, who already had her arms across her chest and glared at the father. "It's not like I was given any choice, when your pirates took over the ship just to get to me," she snapped. "Or maybe I did, but I chose your son over everybody else."

His eyes were glacial, but he nodded. "It is only my son who matters."

"No," she said. "Your wife matters. Your five daughters matter. The child your wife now carries matters."

The husband gasped and turned to look at his wife. The mother nodded tearfully. Immediately he enclosed her in his arms and turned to Abby. "What sex is the baby?"

"I don't know, and I don't care," she said adamantly.

"We don't live in a world where only men have value."

He glared at her. Again.

She wasn't giving an inch. Jax stepped up and said, "The sex of your unborn child is not the issue. Your son here is the issue."

The father nodded. Then he turned to look at Danny, who at this moment in time remained silent, standing off to the side. "Who are you?"

Abby stepped forward. "A specialist who I called in to help me with my diagnosis."

"We already have a diagnosis," he said with a wave of his hand. "It's stomach cancer."

She caught Danny's stifled response. "It's not cancer," she said to Nahim.

He stared at her, and then hope entered his eyes. "If it's not cancer, then you can cure it, can't you?"

Danny said, "Maybe, but in some ways, cancer might be easier to cure."

"Why? What's wrong?" asked the father. There was a tick in his jawline, flickering back and forth, as he waited anxiously for the diagnosis.

"It's attempted murder," Jax said flatly.

Abby nodded. "Somebody's been poisoning your son with arsenic for the last three months."

CHAPTER 13

ALONE IN A waiting room off to the side, Abby sagged into one of the three chairs and eyed the couch along the opposite wall longingly.

"Go lay down if you want," Jax said.

She shook her head. "No, I'll sleep then."

"Maybe that's the best thing for you," Danny said. "I don't understand all the nuances here, but obviously something pretty horrific happened for this to come about."

Jax filled him in, carefully leaving out a few details.

When he was done, Danny sagged in his chair too, his face pale and sweat forming on his forehead. "So am I in danger?"

"If you are, you have my eternal regrets," Abby said. "But I don't think you're in any more danger than any other specialist in this hospital. And as long as Nahim's son is alive, we're all good. But, if his son doesn't make it, then I don't know what'll happen."

"They shot four civilians on the cruise just to get a hold of Abby?"

Jax nodded. "Worse than that, Dr. Benjamin Windberg is involved." He glanced at Abby. "Does Danny know about him?"

She turned toward Danny and said, "Remember in med school when I was having that problem with a stalker?"

"And he attacked you, and you ended up in a hospital with a couple broken bones, a black eye, and a busted nose. Yeah. Hell, I remember that. Why? What's that got to do with this?"

Jax grabbed her in the meantime and said, "What? You didn't tell me about that."

She waved both men off and said, "I'm feeling like a punching bag already right now, so don't make this corner into a boxing ring. I'll come out fighting." She looked at Danny and said, "Yes, that's him. He left the country while out on bail. He went on to do some other work, and I don't know where or what, but apparently he kept watching what I was doing. Then planned that cruise ship bullshit, and I think he's the one poisoning the boy to get me back into his clutches."

Danny stared at her with his jaw opened wide.

"I know," she said. "It makes no sense. But the father would do anything to save his son. I don't doubt that he loves his boy very much. And when Benjamin said I was the only one who could save the boy, the die was cast."

"Holy shit," Danny said. "I wonder about the sanity of Benjamin."

"He's obsessed," she said. "That's all I can say."

"Have you had any contact with him?" Danny asked. "Since he left the country, have you had anything to do with him or seen him at all?"

"Not until this nightmare. But, as you know, my name got into the media a little bit more, and I'm sure, if Benjamin had forgotten about me, that brought me back to his thoughts."

"As if you needed any of that," Danny said. "He's a whack job. Always has been."

"But do you have any proof of that?" Jax said.

Danny shook his head. "Only what Abby's told me."

"Exactly," she said. "I had a lot of threatening phone calls, threatening mail, threatening emails, then he started to follow me home. The tires would be flat on my car when I was at work, and suddenly he'd be there offering me a ride, things like that. But when I was in the living room one night, I saw him with his face pressed against the glass outside my window. When I called the cops, he came back the next night and left me a note, saying I'd be sorry if I told anyone. And he just seemed to get worse at that point.

"So whatever the cops said to him didn't do a damn bit of good. He just carried on stalking me, and finally he entered my house one day. I knew that somebody had been inside. There were notes all over the table and the couch, and there was one on my bed. That was particularly creepy," she said with a shudder. "And the bathtub had been filled, and rose petals were floating inside."

"Oh, my God," Danny said. "I don't know how you survived that."

"Well, I turned around and ran out of the house," she said. "And that's when he caught me. It probably would have been worse if I'd been inside, but, as it was, he caught me outside and was trying to subdue me to take me back inside, and I screamed at the top of my lungs, when he really pounded on me, telling me to shut up, to just shut up." She shook as the memories crowded in on her.

Jax picked her up. She'd been sitting with her knees tucked up against her chest, and he lifted her like a child and put her on his lap. He held her close, and she welcomed the heat radiating from his heavily muscled frame.

"The beating was so bad," she said, "I ended up unconscious and woke up in the hospital. I don't know what he did after that beating. I hate to even think about it. The cops said that they got there and found no sign of anybody else, but I was lying on the sidewalk fully dressed, and the neighbors said that they'd called the cops once they heard me screaming, so everybody presumed he took off. But I wouldn't go back into the house until the cops had been through it. Then I had all the locks changed and added security to all the windows on the lower floor, but I still couldn't live there. I moved soon afterward."

"I don't think I'd ever have gone back in there," Danny said. "That's just horrible."

"And sometimes, in the ensuing years, I looked over my shoulders constantly until I just stopped, and I forgot about it. That's the thing. With the passage of some time, you forget. And then you see him again, and you realize there is just no forgetting some things."

"And he was never charged for the assault?" Danny asked.

"He was released on bail," she said, "and he skipped the country. No way I could get him back to the US because, of course, they'd have picked him up, and that would be it. I didn't know if England would have an extradition treaty or not. I mean, who knows about these things? But I figured just maybe we could do something with him in England if he tried anything."

"I'm sure we can," Jax said quietly. "He shouldn't be allowed to escape from something like that."

"No," she said. "I do have the detective's name, and I do have a copy of the police file and the medical records from his last assault, so, if he ever gets caught here and is sent back to the States, a lot of detectives want to talk to him. For all I know, it could be a case of only three or four months' time in jail. And maybe he can buy his way out of it. Hell, his boss might pay the fine. But surely something like poisoning a child is even worse."

"Assaults like yours shouldn't entail just a fine," Danny said.

She shrugged. "And yet, when he was stalking me, there wasn't anything the authorities could do, they said. I got a court order to keep him away, but it wasn't like anybody'll enforce that. When he comes after you, he comes after you." She sagged against Jax's chest and said, "Women all over the world have had this problem since forever. Until it becomes bad enough, and we're injured, nobody does anything about it."

At that, she could feel Jax's arms tighten convulsively around her. "Well, that asshole will pay before he leaves the country," he said.

"And then you'll get charged," she said sadly. "I can't have that on my conscience."

Danny gave a hoarse laugh. "That's the way you are, isn't it? You're always after the underdog, trying to help the one who needs it the most and never looking after yourself." He shook his head. "You used to do that all the time in med school."

"I know," she said. "It's a problem, and I get that, but it's who I am. It's also why I'm trying to help the boy."

"Well, the boy isn't responsible for his father's actions or for his doctor's, who may very well have poisoned him," Danny said in agreement. "My colleagues and I have some idea what might help Abdul out. But it'll require stem cells and some blood transfusions and a whole lot of luck. He's weak, so it might be too late."

"Well, I'm pretty sure the father will okay anything and everything that's needed."

"I hope so," he said, "because, as soon as I catch a few minutes of rest, and hopefully have the okay on it, we must help this little boy into the OR."

"Will you do it?"

He shook his head. "No, but we have some specialists here who will take it on."

She smiled as he got up and walked to the door. "Wait. I thought you would rest?"

"I decided against it," he said. "The boy doesn't have time for me to take an hour. The sooner we get the stem-cell collecting going, the better." And he disappeared, one of the MI6 agents on his tail.

She looked at Jax and said, "I can't really help him. Do you object to me lying down?"

He raised an eyebrow and said, "No, but I thought you wanted food."

"We're back to that again," she said with a laugh. "I want Abby time first, then food." She had a tired smile on her face as she crawled off his lap and walked to the couch. "This will kill my neck."

"Are there no pillows?" he asked.

She looked around and shrugged. "No, there aren't."

But when she turned around again, he had a stack of towels in his hand. He laid them on the corner beside the armrest and said, "Try that."

She curled up with her feet under one armrest and her head on top of the towels at the other armrest, and, within five minutes, she said, "This feels really good. Good night."

⚓

JAX

JAX WAITED, PONDERING all the information she'd finally given him on Dr. Windberg. The fact that this Benjamin guy had gotten away with what he had done and that the world knew he was still alive and still out there and free as a bird, now to come back after her with such devastating consequences, just blew Jax away. Sure, Benjamin had been released on bail and then had skipped the country, but had nobody bothered to track him down?

Crimes like this made Jax so angry. She was vulnerable to anything and everyone out there because of her size, her sex, and her profession even made her a target from those willing to take what they wanted, instead of getting the things in life that were earned. And it didn't matter if Nahim really cared about Abdul because, in this case, so many people had already paid the price. Jax wanted to see how things were progressing but didn't dare leave her.

The door opened, and Beau walked in. He started to speak but saw her sleeping on the couch and smiled. "She looks like a two-year-old," he said affectionately.

"I'm sure she'd be insulted by that," Jax said with a chuckle. "At least a six-year-old."

"Not much more. But I need food, and I think Danny is looking for food. When she wakes, she'll need to eat too."

"What's happening with the boy?"

"They're taking him to the OR for the stem-cell work."

"Good," Jax said. "I was afraid the father would object."

"No, not at all. But he's still hammering to find out the sex of the child his wife's carrying."

"He doesn't deserve to have another child," Jax said with fatigue in his voice. "Not if he ordered his security guards to kill those people on the cruise. There were so many easier ways to snag Abby."

"But it's a godsend that he did it this way because that allowed us to get her first."

Jax thought about that, then nodded. "I'll give you a point there."

"I've ordered food," Beau said. "That's what I really came in to tell you. You've got about fifteen to twenty minutes, and then it'll be delivered."

"And no sign of Benjamin?"

Beau shook his head. "I've checked in with Jonas a couple times and Griffin too. There's been no sighting anywhere after Benjamin's initial arrival and subsequent disappearance. We're all on alert."

"That's worse than having him on the premises."

"It is," Beau said. "And I know Jonas is not happy either. He doesn't want this guy loose in the UK."

"I know," Jax said. Then he repeated what Abby had said about her injuries.

Beau sat down on the other chair where Danny had been sitting and stared at him. "And they didn't arrest him on the spot?"

"Well, they did find him and arrest him but then released him on bail," Jax said. "And, of course, he didn't show up for his court date."

"That's just an invitation to take off though," Beau said. "That's disgusting."

"I know," Jax said. "I'm trying to figure out how to make sure he doesn't get away with it now. There's not a whole lot we can do about it, except finding something here that might encourage the British government to keep him."

"Like Jonas said, that leaves them paying the costs of keeping an American criminal."

"Sure," Jax said, "but they can always trade him back

over again. It happens all the time."

"Unfortunately it does. Not only that, if you think about it, so many people are out-of-country, paying for crimes that they committed in their own country."

"Well, as long as we stop this asshole," Jax said with some heat, "I don't care which country he ends up jailed in."

"Let's hope that maybe this guy gets a *permanent* sentence," Beau said as he glanced back at Abby. "She doesn't deserve this."

"No, she doesn't," Jax said. "She's doing everything she can here to make the situation better, but she's struggling, knowing Benjamin is out there somewhere, planning."

"It's the *out there somewhere* part," Beau said, "that really worries me."

"I know. She keeps turning around, looking for him. Watching her, it seems she feels like somebody's watching her today."

"The trouble is, everybody is. Literally everybody is watching her."

"Well, Danny seems to be a good guy for her to have called," Jax said.

"Right. I really like him," Beau said. "And he's marshaled the medical team together. So, with any luck, we might save the kid."

"Doesn't change the fact that somebody's been poisoning the kid. Abby thinks it's Benjamin."

"Sure, but that's who she wants to be guilty," Beau said. "We can't allow that to be the given answer. We must make sure that it's the right answer. I admit that I'd like it to be him too because then I'm pretty sure the father will take him out."

"I'm pretty sure he will too," Jax said with a grin. "Solves all of our problems."

"But Benjamin will probably prove that it was somebody else. And he's pretty slippery."

"I'm betting that he'll say it's the head of security," Jax said. "To cause dissent within the family unit as well."

"Family unit?"

"The head of security, Bahan, is the father's brother."

"Ah," Beau said. "That'd be a really good fall guy."

"I wish to God somebody would find Benjamin though."

Just then a phone buzzed. Beau pulled out his, checked it, and said, "Food's here."

Just then Jax got a buzz too. "And that's Griffin checking in."

"You don't have to answer it," Beau said. "We all are on our own."

"I know," Jax said. "But, if he can get eyes on Benjamin, that would help." He quickly sent a text to that effect and then put away his phone. "Benjamin's slippery," Jax said.

"He's too slippery," Beau said. "You watch your back. I'll go get the food." And he got up and walked out.

Needing a bit of fresh air, Jax opened up both windows and checked to make sure there was no way that anybody could get in through the third-story windows. Satisfied, he then walked back to the door and opened it and leaned against the doorjamb, his arms crossed over his chest as he watched the comings and goings. One of the easiest ways for Benjamin to get in the damn hospital would be in scrubs or a lab coat. He was a goddamn doctor. What was to stop him from snagging a white coat and just walking around like he knew the place? As a camouflage, it was one of the best possible ways he could infiltrate the hospital. And that bothered Jax.

Surely somebody would be checking the video cameras. He wasn't sure about that though and quickly sent a second message out, this time to Jonas, asking for somebody to keep an eye on the video feeds. He got an immediate response back.

We know how to do our job.

Jax snorted. "Sure you do." But, in all fairness, he didn't know how bad things were out there, in the hospital or in all of London either. For all he knew, it wasn't bad at all. As he stood here, he watched Beau through the glass doors, walking toward him with two large bags in his hand. Several people talked and joked with him. He just smiled, didn't answer, and kept on going. When he caught up to Jax, he handed over the bags and said, "I'll go find Danny. He needs to eat too."

Jax nodded. "And come back in and eat something yourself." He placed the bags on the table and returned to the open door. Soon enough Danny and Beau joined him.

Danny lifted his nose and smiled. "That smells like fish and chips."

Beau shrugged. "For Abby."

Just then she stirred on the couch. She opened her eyes, stared up at Beau, and her nostrils flared. "Oh, my God," she said. "Is that fish and chips?"

Beau chuckled. "I do believe that was your request."

She slowly got to her feet, saw the bags and Danny, and walked over. "I'm still half asleep," she said. "And it doesn't matter. I'll eat anyway."

"Ha," Jax said. "How about going to the washroom and washing your hands and face first? You'll feel better."

She nodded. "I could do that." She headed to the door,

and Jax immediately hopped up behind her. "I can go alone, you know."

"You might," he said, "but you won't. Because I'll be with you every step of the way."

"Not in the stall you're not," she snapped.

He shrugged. "Then don't do anything stupid that makes me think I have to be there too."

She glared at him and turned to Beau, who had a smirk on his face. "Don't you dare laugh at that."

Beau just looked at her and said, "Remember? This is all about your safety."

She sighed and walked out. Jax followed her to the women's washroom, where she pushed open the door. Several other women were inside. She smiled at Jax and said, "I should be safe enough."

He frowned and didn't like it one bit when she shut the door in his face.

CHAPTER 14

INSIDE THE BATHROOM, she quickly used the facilities, walked over to the sink, lathered up good, cleaned her arms and her hands, and then went at her face. She should have brought a brush with her. But she dropped the clip from her hair and then quickly ran her fingers through and put the clip back in. There wasn't a whole lot she could do about the rest of her, but food would hopefully help with the exhausted look in her eyes. She opened the door and stepped out. Only she saw no sign of Jax. She looked around and again couldn't find him. Confused and a little worried, she pulled out her phone and called Beau.

"What's the matter? You missed me? I figured, with Jax around, you wouldn't even see me."

"That's the problem," she said. "There's no Jax."

"Where are you?" Beau asked an alarm.

"Standing at the women's washroom," she said. "I walked in and shut the door in his face because it was full of women."

"How long ago?"

"I don't know," she said, bewildered. "Maybe five minutes, eight?"

"Put your phone away," he snapped.

She looked down at her phone, then looked up to see Beau striding toward her. She stared up at him. "Where could he be?"

"I'm not sure," he said, but he was already dialing his phone. He snapped out orders to somebody on the other end and then turned around and assessed all the closest doors. "No way somebody would have carried an unconscious Jax very far, and he would have to be unconscious before he left you."

There were two doors across the hall. He quickly walked over to one. It was locked, and the other one was open. He checked the open one first, then crossed back over to the same side as the women's washroom and checked it. Both were empty. He headed over to the locked door, pulled something from his back pocket, and quickly popped the lock on the door.

She gasped. "You shouldn't do that. There could be a patient in there."

"And there could be a dead Jax in there," he snapped.

Instantly she fell silent, her heart slamming against her chest as she thought about that. "It better not be," she cried out.

"Well, let's hope not," he said as he stepped inside.

She heard his exclamation as he went farther into the room, and she raced in behind him. Jax was collapsed on the floor. She raced over and checked for a pulse, ecstatic that he was still alive. Breathing heavily, she quickly did as much of a check of him as she could. "Oh, my God," she said. "He's alive, but it looks like he's been hit over the head."

"Yes, how is he though?"

She smacked him lightly on the cheeks. "Jax, wake up. Wake up."

He woke up and looked at her and then frowned. "What happened?"

"What happened," she said, "was you got taken out."

He stared at her in horror, jumped to his feet, and forcibly stopped. He looked at Beau and then at her and said, "Are you two okay?"

"Yes. Do you remember what happened?"

Jax frowned and said, "You turned. You shut the door on my face. Then I turned around …" And then he shook his head. "Something came out of nowhere and smacked me in the head."

"How busy was the washroom?" Beau asked.

"Too damn busy," she snapped. "There were at least four or five women. After I came out of the stall, it was pretty well empty though."

"So nobody was there?"

"Two women came in as I stepped out," she said. "Both in scrubs and talking and laughing. I had to wait for them to get out of the doorway so I could leave."

"So Benjamin was probably hoping to come in while you were in there, but, with the women coming through, it would be too many for him to deal with."

"We need the video feed," Jax said.

"I've already got Jonas looking at it," Beau said.

"Great," Jax said. "He'll never let me forget this one."

"That's hardly the point," she said, glaring at him. "We can't take any chances. This guy's now attacked you. So we must make sure that Abdul and his family are okay."

"Everybody is looking for Benjamin now, and MI6 has more men on Abdul's family," Beau said. "Let's get you back to the room, Abby."

"Oh, my God, did you leave Danny alone?"

"Don't worry. One MI6 agent is on him at all times." Beau nodded. "I left him eating fish and chips."

"Just one guard?" Abby asked.

They raced down the hallway and burst into the room. Danny looked up. "Damn, I was hoping you guys weren't coming back," he complained good-naturedly. "I was really hoping to get another piece of fish."

She sagged down on a chair. "Somebody attacked Jax," she said, her voice faint. She rubbed her face. "I was in the washroom, stepped out, and he wasn't there."

"Seriously?" Danny asked.

Jax nodded and said, "Yeah, I've got a hell of a headache." He touched the sore spot, and, when he came away, his fingers were coated in blood.

She stared at it and said, "So either we fix that wound now or after we eat. I vote for after we eat."

He stared at her. "What kind of doctor are you who wouldn't look at it first?" he asked in mock outrage.

She sent him a cheeky grin. "While you were unconscious—on the floor, flaked out from fainting, or possibly from seeing the blood—I already checked it over. It just needs a good wash and maybe a bandage."

Beau chuckled.

Jax glared at her. "I did not faint, and I do not faint at the sight of blood."

"Could have fooled me," she said. "For all I know, you and head wounds are just a thing."

"What does that mean?" he asked.

"It means that you are a baby when you get hurt. And you get injured a lot."

"I'm not a baby when I get hurt," he said. "And how dare you even say that."

She shrugged. "You know what? People talk all the time, but that doesn't really mean anything. It's how you act when under duress—like vomiting at the sight of blood."

He groaned. "What got into you all of a sudden? ... Whatever—anything to make it easier for you right now," he said with a snort.

"Anything to make it easier for me? I'm not the one who got taken down while on the job," she said with a chuckle.

He just glared at her and grabbed the largest piece of fish. "For that, I'll steal all the food."

"Well, you might try," she said, snagging it from his fingers and taking a great big bite.

He stared at his empty fingers and then at her in astonishment.

Beau laughed. "See? I told you that you two are great together."

Instantly both of them turned and glared at him.

He raised both hands in surrender. "You know what? I can stay quiet for a little bit, but it's obvious what's going on."

She glanced at Danny, and he nodded. "It's very obvious."

She rolled her eyes at him.

"I'm so happy for you," he said.

"Don't be. He's not very easy to get along with."

"Maybe not," he said, "but you obviously know how to handle him."

At that, she dug into her fish and chips and didn't speak again until she finally finished. And that was to push the remainder of her plate away from her and say, "Okay. I'm so done."

"Maybe," Jax said, "but you're never really done when it comes to food. Could be all kinds of things that you'll need later."

"Maybe, but that's later," she said. "I can't do anything more now."

"Okay," he said. "Then I'll finish yours too." And he snagged the half piece of fish and the last few chips off her plate.

She chuckled. "Well, I'm glad to see that you're feeling better."

"I never said I wasn't."

"No," she said. "Obviously not. The thing is, we still haven't heard from anybody searching the hospital's security video to know who hit you."

"Not quite true," Beau said. "It was your Benjamin." He picked up his phone, brought up a screenshot that he had been sent, and held it up for her. And there was Benjamin dressed in a white doctor's jacket with a stethoscope around his neck.

"How cliché," she murmured. "You can still hide the devil doing the angel's work."

"Maybe," he said, "but our world and our entire purpose right now is to make sure we take down this guy. He attacked one of us. He doesn't get away with that again."

"Maybe, but he already did once."

"I know," Beau said, "but we'll get him. The hospital has been alerted that he's already inside and that he has attacked somebody."

She nodded, her face grim. "Doesn't mean it'll change anything though."

"Oh, ye of little faith," Beau said.

"No," she said. "I know this guy. And he's something else."

"Maybe," Beau said, "but you must admit Jax and I have kept you safe so far."

"But maybe I should be keeping Jax safe," she said with a smirk.

"How about we both look after each other?" Jax asked, his temper rising. He leaned over and kissed her quickly on the cheek. "I'd hate to leave you now."

"True," she said, getting melancholy. "You guys have done a great job looking after me."

"So let's stay strong," he said.

"I will," she said, "but I think Beau needs to look after both of us." With that cheeky comment, she got up, walked to the food bags, and pulled out bottles of water. "Look at this. The only thing we're missing is some coffee."

"If you're ready for coffee," Beau said, "we can order it. I wanted to make sure you got food in you first. The last thing you need is a caffeine hit on an empty stomach."

"Are you sure? Still, my stomach is so far from empty right now …"

Just then Danny's pager went off, and he held it up and said, "I've got to go to the OR. I want to see what they're up to. I asked them to tag me when we got to this stage."

"Good," she said. "Do you want me to come?"

He shook his head. "Better you stay safe," he said. "And keep these guys out of trouble." He laughed and headed out.

She frowned and hopped to the door, Jax getting up behind her as she stood in the hallway and waited until Danny and his MI6 guard safely turned in the direction of surgery. "I want you to go after him," she said. "Make sure he gets there safe."

"That's nice," Jax said, his arms across his chest. "I'm not going anywhere. The next time you go to the bathroom, I'm going inside with you."

She gasped. "You can't do that."

He turned, gave her a hard look, and said, "Watch me."

⚓

AND JAX MEANT every word. Abby would not get more than four inches away from him again. He couldn't believe he'd been taken out, and it would piss him off for a long time. The fact of the matter is, the guy had every opportunity to kill him and hadn't. And why not? Had Benjamin been disturbed or could he have just left a line of women in the hallway? What was it he wanted to use Jax as? Collateral to keep her compliant? He didn't know what the reason was, but he would make damn sure that this guy wouldn't get a second chance. He knew Beau could feel the seething anger underneath his skin, whereas she appeared to be completely oblivious to it. And maybe that was okay too. But it was Jax's job, and the fact is, he'd been taken out and that was something that would never, ever go over well.

"Ease up," Beau said. "I'll walk down and make sure that Danny arrived okay." His long legs ate up the hallway until he turned and followed Danny's direction.

Abby sighed and turned to look at Jax. "I shouldn't tease you because the bottom line was that, while Benjamin was busy taking you out, he couldn't be taking me out. For that, I'm grateful and very sad that you got hurt." And she reached out, cupped his face gently, and kissed him on the lips. Then she threw her arms around him and hugged him tightly.

Instantly his arms came around her, and he held her close. "I'm just so damn pissed that he got me in the first place," he muttered against her hair.

She nodded, strands of long chestnut hair flying loose from the clip and floating across his face. "I get that," she said. "And it didn't seem to matter how much I ever did to hide from Benjamin. He always seemed to find me. And that's what he's done again now."

What he heard here was a sense of defeat already and a sense of victimization, as if knowing that she could do nothing to get away from Benjamin. And with Benjamin taking Jax out himself once, it just confirmed her belief that this guy was better than anyone, if not a little bit supernatural in his methods.

"We'll get him," he said calmly. "Don't you worry about it."

"I know you believe that," she said. "And I really want to too. But he's just not quite the same as the rest of us."

"No," Jax said, still holding her close. "He's broken. There's something wrong with him. But that doesn't mean he can get away with doing this shit."

When Beau hadn't come back by now, she turned, looked down the hallway, and said, "Surely nobody will go after him. Will they?"

Just then Jax's phone buzzed in his pocket. He pulled it out and found a message from Beau.

Am I bringing coffee back?

He hit Dial and put it on Speaker. When Beau answered, Jax said, "I figured she needed to hear your voice. She was worried when you didn't come back right away."

Beau's beautiful laughter rolled through the phone. "I'm fine," he said. "You might want to consider that somebody's got to be my size to cause the same damage he did to Jax. It'll take another really big guy to bring me down."

"No," Abby said sharply. "A bullet will do the job in a nanosecond."

Silence. "Wow, you got a point," Beau said. "But do you

want coffee with cream or sugar?"

"I want a latte," she said. "No sugar and make it as large as you can get."

"Done. Back in five."

"And stay safe," she snapped sharply into the phone at Beau as Jax held it up.

"I will," Beau said gently. "You look after him."

And on that note, he chuckled and hung up.

Jax rolled his eyes.

"He'll really get a lot of mileage out of that, won't he?" she asked.

"No way he won't."

"Good," she said. "It helps to keep things a little bit lighter right now."

"True," he said. "At the same time, we can't have things so easy that we forget."

She nodded. "We can't return to the hotel tonight, can we?"

He shrugged.

Just as they stood here, a man strode toward them.

Jax said, "Oh, oh, don't look now but here comes the head of security."

"That asshole," she said, separating from Jax and turning to look. She stiffened, crossed her arms over her chest, and glared at the man as he approached.

He just looked at her, dismissed her as not important, then glanced at Jax. "I hear you were attacked," he said smoothly.

"Funny how word gets around like that," Jax said. "So, where were you?"

The man's eyebrows shot up. "Down with Abdul's father and his mother. There are video cameras everywhere that will clear me."

Unfortunately there were. Jax just didn't have word as to who'd been cleared and who hadn't yet. Jax nodded and said, "Hopefully they will. And we haven't forgotten that you shot those people on the cruise ship."

"And again, at my brother's orders," he said smoothly.

"Why are you here?" Abby asked.

"Abdul's father, my brother, would like to talk to you."

"Why? I told him that it was arsenic poisoning and that somebody was trying to murder Abdul."

"Yes. Obviously he wants to discuss that further. But, more than that, he wants to know who tried to kill his son." When she didn't move, he added, "Now," and promptly left.

CHAPTER 15

Abby so didn't want to talk to Nahim. He was the man who had orchestrated the takeover of the cruise ship, all to get at her, and she would never forgive him for that excessive use of force—killing four innocent passengers—when a simple and commonsense request could have been made instead. She looked at Jax. "What do you think?"

He reached an arm around her shoulder, tucking her up close.

She appreciated his instinctive knowledge of how she felt because it sucked. Like, it really sucked to always be afraid.

He nodded and said, "I think it's time that we had a talk with Nahim."

She didn't really agree, but it was probably the best thing to do in the circumstances. She didn't always agree with the way things were handled. What else was new? Together, they all walked to where Nahim waited for news from the work being done inside the OR. He stood, his facial expression very different from the first time she'd met him. In that initial face-to-face with him, she felt as if she were some rare specimen to crawl out from underneath the carpet. But, right now, his focus on her was more direct. "My son is slowly being murdered?" he asked. "What do you know of this?"

"I know that arsenic was fed to him slowly and steadily over time," she admitted readily. "As to who, I have no proof."

Nahim looked down at his wife. "Very few people are close to him."

"So you immediately accuse your wife?" she asked, her voice steadfast. Jax had kept his arm around her shoulder, silent in his support. And she appreciated it. He wasn't trying to disagree with her viewpoint or tell her not to do her thing but just stood here, letting her talk to the father.

"I am not blaming her," Nahim argued. "But she's responsible for his food."

"Sure," Abby said. "But many *other* people have access, including yourself."

Immediately his nostrils flared, and his voice sharpened. "You think that I would hurt my son?"

"I don't know," she said. "Would you? Do you have life insurance on him? Maybe you already know that she carries a second son, so the first one's a spare."

His ire rose, as his fists clenched tighter. He took a step forward.

Only Jax was waiting. "You will not come any closer," he said quietly.

Nahim's gaze darted in Jax's direction, then back at her. "You cannot expect to accuse me of murder or trying to hurt my son like that and not expect me to respond."

"I'm glad you responded as you did, with emotions, maybe with honesty," she said simply. "Maybe you are not responsible. But it doesn't change the fact that someone administered the poison. Over three consecutive months. Whether that was you, your brother, or somebody else, like his medical physician"—she paused long enough so that Nahim could really assimilate her words—"isn't for me to decipher. But I won't allow you to blame your wife."

"How was that not for you to decipher?" he asked. "You cannot throw around accusations like that."

"I don't care to," she said. "I am much more concerned about the fact that your little boy is suffering, and he doesn't need to be, and this must be stopped."

Nahim shook his head. "On what do you base these charges?"

"They're not my charges. The medical tests prove it," she said. "All I can tell you is that your son was systematically fed arsenic. It's up to you to determine who closest to you is trying to hurt you through killing your son."

He stared at her and tilted his chin, as if finally considering her words, and then glanced at Jax.

Jax waited.

She asked Nahim, "Who has the most to gain if your son dies? Who has the most to gain if you die without an heir?" His gaze widened, and she nodded. "Who has the most to gain if something in your family blows up like this? Outside of causing you and your wife massive pain, what else does it do?"

"It disrupts the lineage," he admitted. "The power would return to my brother."

"Return?" Jax asked.

"I'm the second-born son, but Father deemed me to take over for him."

"But only if you die, correct?"

Nahim nodded.

The head of security stepped forward. "I don't like you implying that I would kill my brother to take his place," he snapped. "We made peace over this many years ago. He is my boss and always will be."

"Until he's not here anymore," she said quite calmly.

"But it may not have anything to do with you, Nahim, or your brother. You might also want to consider why I was supposedly brought in to help treat your son."

"You were the best, the doctor said. Although I don't see how this is. You are a woman. And you are young."

She snorted. "I'm the best at what I do," she said. "Your son does not have cancer. So that doctor already misdiagnosed Abdul's condition. There was no need for me to look after your son."

"So you're saying that he's a poor doctor? This, I was wondering."

"Because your son wasn't getting any better?"

"And, in many ways, he was getting worse. Nothing seemed to help stop his downward slide."

"Did Dr. Windberg see your son before you hired him as the full-time doctor for you and your family?"

Nahim nodded. "I interviewed several doctors, and each of them did a full exam of Abdul."

"So it's possible that Dr. Windberg could have administered some arsenic at the time, making your son greatly ill. Then, when you brought Windberg back on, your son was already very sick, and he just helped his condition deteriorate to this point."

"And yet, there is no reason for that," he said.

"Except for the fact that you didn't bring in Dr. Windberg as your first choice, did you?" she asked. Because now she wondered about something else.

He looked at her, frowned, and then said, "You can't know this."

She nodded slowly. "Dr. Windberg thought for sure, his ego being what it is, that you would immediately bring him back as the primary physician for your family. At that point in time, he might have done much to help your son. And maybe the condition that Abdul suffered from earlier wasn't all that bad. I can't know because I'm not privy to all that's gone on. But, if Windberg administered arsenic at the time of his interview, thinking he'd be back within a few days, he could have easily helped your son recover. But, when you didn't bring Windberg back immediately, I think his attitude changed. He knew that you had another first choice for your primary physician—or a second or even a third. And likely he kept administering the arsenic as a punishment to you."

"That makes no sense," Nahim said with a wave of his hand. "You're not giving us any proof. These are fabrications and lies."

"Could be, sure," she said. "My theory could be wrong because I don't have a complete and true set of facts here. And, yes, I want it to be Dr. Windberg because I have a predisposition to hate him—rightly earned as he attacked me and put me in the hospital. But I also don't want you to be taken in by his lies."

Nahim frowned at her. "What does this mean?" He looked at his head of security and back at her. But Jax stepped up and explained the scenario.

Nahim's eyes widened. "I know nothing of this," he exclaimed. "That is not allowed in our culture."

"It's not allowed in ours either," she said. "Windberg needs to return to the US, where they're waiting for him, but instead we're here in England."

"And he is here too."

"I know," she said. "I saw him. And I think he is watching me. I wonder if this whole thing wasn't to bring me back into his clutches."

Nahim studied her up and down and then shrugged, as

if to say it made no sense to him.

She didn't want to take it as a personal insult, but it was such an odd feeling to know that she had been checked over and dismissed as not even worthy. She laughed. "I'm grateful for your response, but I wish Benjamin had the same."

"I will ask him," Nahim said. "But it is highly unlikely he would do anything like this for a woman. Women are easy and cheap."

"Sure," Abby said in a dry tone. "In your world. I wonder how your wife feels about that." She glanced over to see the woman.

Her face was carefully blank as she sat on a chair, having nothing to say, of course.

He glanced at her and then back at Abby. "We still must know the sex of the child."

"And you will know the sex of the child when it's born," she said carefully. "I won't encourage your prejudices as to whatever sex is the child she's carrying."

He glared at her.

She shrugged. "Neither will we chintz on the care of your son, as you think that maybe it's okay for him to die because a second son may be on the way."

He just shook his head. "I would do no such thing."

"Right," she said. "I do believe you about Abdul." But she stood here and stared at him with such disdain on her face that she knew he got the message.

He drew himself up to his full height and said, "I do not like you."

"I do not like you," she retorted immediately.

He looked shocked at that. "Why?"

"Because you treat your wife like dirt. Because you allowed people to hurt your son. Because you used brute force to engage my services when a simple phone call would do. And, even now, all you care about is making sure you have *another* son on the way."

"I *must* have a son," he roared.

"Or what?"

"We have discussed this," he said. "Or the order goes to my brother."

"So maybe your brother gets to rule. But does he have a son?"

Nahim looked at his brother and then nodded reluctantly. "He has four sons."

"So the family's lineage is safe," she said carefully. "It's just not the way you wanted it to be." She could see that it made Nahim extremely distraught to even consider such a thing. "Besides," she said, "your wife is carrying another child, and your son is still alive."

He nodded. "And, for that, I must keep him alive. She has already given birth to five girls. I need more boys."

"Maybe," Abby said. "But since your sperm determines the sex of the child, that's hardly her fault." He didn't like hearing that. She wasn't sure if he'd ever been told that in his life. She studied him. "Did you not know that?"

"I know that," he muttered. "But, according to our ways, she can do things to make it one way or the other."

"Oh, brother," she said. "Please spare me that drivel. *Your sperm* decides the sex of the child. That's it. So, if you are only producing daughters, it is you who needs to be questioning your own contribution to your family hierarchy. The fact that you have produced one son means that at least you *can* produce a son. Now all you must do is produce more."

"Yes," he admitted.

Just then Danny came back into the room. He caught sight of Abby and smiled. "I'm cautiously optimistic," he said. "The process went well. Now it'll just be a matter of time." He looked at the mother and asked, "Do you want to be with him?"

Immediately her face broke into a smile, and Abby could see the tears in her eyes. The mother raced to Danny, and he led her away.

The father stood, staring at Abby. "Why am I not allowed to see my son?"

"You are," she said. "Do you want me to take you to him?"

He hesitated, then nodded. "Yes, please."

She immediately followed Danny and Abdul's mother until both parents were at their son's side. She watched as Nahim leaned over, gently stroking a finger across the boy's temple. The child shifted, looked up at his father, and smiled. And, if she hadn't been looking quite so closely, she wouldn't have seen the sheen of tears in Nahim's eyes.

It was good to see. She really did want to believe that Nahim cared about his son because the other possibility was that, for whatever twisted reason, he had administered the arsenic himself. She stepped back and watched the family tableau. The head of security stood slightly to the side. She caught a glimpse of his expression, and she wondered if he cared at all. She walked closer and, in a low voice, said, "The child will live. Better luck next time." And she walked past him.

He grabbed her arm and shook her hard. "Woman, you stay silent in my presence," he roared.

Immediately Jax decked him, dropping Nahim's brother to his knees, while surely his head rang, his brain shaking inside his skull, gasping until the pain stopped. Nahim was there instantly. "What is the meaning of this?"

Jax responded tightly. "He attacked Abby. That will never be allowed in any country."

Nahim looked down at his brother and said, "What's wrong with you?"

"She implied I'm the one responsible."

"Well, if Nahim can blame his wife," she said, "then I might as well blame you too."

"Why is that?" he asked as he slowly made his way to his feet.

"Because she can't look after all aspects of Abdul's safety. You are the head of security for all of the family. So you've failed to do your job."

And, on that note, she turned and walked away.

⚓

"I'D LIKE TO speak with you," Jax said to Nahim, "but I must keep an eye on her."

"Why is she in danger?" asked Nahim in confusion. "I will keep my brother away from her."

"That would be good," he said, "but the fact that you ordered your brother to kill four innocent people in order to grab her, that'll never go down in her books."

Nahim drew himself up to his full height and said, "We were prepared to do what was necessary. I did not know about the shootings though. They were not done by my orders."

"And how about now? Your son doesn't have cancer, and you didn't need Abby at all," Jax said. "So on whose orders were those deceptions done?" He called out, "Abby, stop."

She froze, turned, and glared at him. "Hurry up then."

Jax turned back to Nahim. "You should speak to your family's primary doctor who made an incorrect diagnosis and who caused all this chaos."

"He said that he had an incorrect diagnosis from the previous doctor," Nahim said cautiously. "And that he needed this woman."

"And even you must see how ridiculous his explanation is."

At that, Nahim nodded. "Yes, yes. I can see that."

"Finally one point made that we agree upon." She groaned, came up to him, and said, "Talk to Windberg. Why you left him in charge of getting me when all you had to do was phone me is absurd. So ask Windberg about that charade on the cruise ship to get a hold of me. Why not just send a couple men on board to take me from my cabin and move me at any one of the port stops? Or why not stop me before I got on the ship or even from my hometown?" She shook her head. "Instead you created an international incident and terrified thousands of people and killed four. For what?" she asked with a disparaging snort. "For a worthless doctor your son doesn't even need. So ask yourself, why did Windberg do this?"

But the father already had his phone out and dialed someone. "Benjamin, where are you? I must speak with you," he said, then paused, seemingly listening to Benjamin on the other line. "Regardless, I want you at the hospital waiting room. The first stage of treatment has been done for my son, but I need to talk to you." And without giving him any chance, he hung up. "Now Benjamin will come," he said. "And we will get answers."

"Good," she said. "In the meantime, I want a cup of coffee." She turned to leave, only to face the head of security standing at the end of the hallway. "Jax?" she said.

"I see him," Jax said easily, then turned toward Nahim. "Do you really expect to stop us from leaving?"

Nahim shook his head. "No. I don't want that. But I do want Benjamin here so that he can see and address your accusations himself."

"Perfect," Jax said. "But did you ever ask Benjamin if he's interested in being here with the rest of us?"

Nahim frowned. "Of course he would be," he said. "Every man wants to meet his accusers."

"Ah, if you say so," Jax said. "The thing is, I don't really believe Windberg agrees with you on that."

"We'll see then, won't we?" he said. "He is on his way."

"Good," Jax said. "How long will it take him?"

"It won't take him long at all."

Thirty minutes later, there was still no sign of Benjamin. Jax and Abby leaned against the hall wall, not seeing anybody. He could feel the tension in Abby's frame as she waited for the man of her nightmares to show up. But the longer it went on, she turned to Nahim and finally said, "I don't think he'll show."

"He will show," he said. "He must show."

"And why is that?" she asked.

"Because I've ordered him to come," he said in surprise. "He has no choice."

"Interesting," she said. "So where is he then?"

He pulled out his phone and called Benjamin. "There's no answer," he said, frowning.

The head of security said, "But we're not allowed to use phones much in the hospital, so he may have turned his off."

Nahim nodded. "That makes sense."

"No," Jax said. "It does not make sense."

"You are not being fair," the security man said.

"Maybe not," Jax said, "but we're quite prepared to sit here and wait."

And wait they did for another forty-five minutes, and now Nahim grew angrier. He motioned at his brother and said, "Go find him." Immediately he took off.

"My brother does not like you implying that he is trying to take me out."

"Of course he doesn't," she said. "Nobody would like that. The fact of the matter is, somebody has been administering arsenic to your son. *For three whole months*. Who has that kind of daily access to Abdul? If it's not you—and I do not believe it's your wife or the child's grandmother—then who?"

Nahim studied her for a long moment and then gave a clipped nod. "That's the question, isn't it? Then who?"

She nodded. "My bet is on Benjamin."

"But you are already prejudiced against this man," he protested.

"With good reason," she said. "Who arranged the plans for the cruise ship?"

"Benjamin and my brother arranged it."

"And you did not think there was an easier way?"

He shrugged. "I did not care. My son was dying. Anything that will save him was fine."

"Got it," she said. "So your family rates over all other families."

"As it would be for you as well, if it was your family."

He had a point, Abby thought. Because everybody would consider themselves and their families as a high priority when it came to some crunch like this.

"The question is, who else had access?" Jax asked.

"I do not know," Nahim stated. "It should have been nobody. That is why we set it up as it is."

"Were you expecting an attack on your son?" Jax asked.

"There was always a possibility," he said. "I have enemies. And I am wealthy. That always brings in trouble."

"Exactly," Jax said. "But it's rarely as complicated as that. Somebody has to be *very* close to Abdul in order to access the child to give daily doses of the poison."

The father nodded. "So I understand. It leaves me with very few suspects."

"Exactly," she said. "Definitely a few things need to be considered."

"Agreed." He considered her intently. "Why do you not want to be with the doctor? It's a prestigious position, and he makes good money. Many women want him."

"Because he hurts me," she said. "Because I don't like him, and I don't believe he is good doctor. And he's certainly not a good man."

Nahim frowned. "I am not happy to hear this."

"No," she said. "I imagine you're not. But you have Windberg looking after your son, and you should take another look at that."

"Who cleared him for this position?" Jax asked.

"My brother," he said, "but Benjamin had been a physician for another family member."

"And did their child live?"

"Yes, he got very ill, and this doctor helped."

"Good," she said. "As long as Benjamin didn't cause the illness in the first place."

Nahim stared at her, his eyes going dark as he mentally

went through a time frame. "I don't know," he said. "He got sick after the doctor arrived, but then the doctor fixed him."

"Exactly," she said. "It often happens that way so that a doctor can build himself a great reputation."

"They deliberately make somebody sick so they can heal them?" Nahim asked in shock.

"People like Benjamin, of course," she said. "But, in your son's case, something went wrong. And that's why Windberg wanted help. This is a different kind of medicine."

"But we have this kind of medicine, don't we?"

"That's a question you really must ask yourself because I do not know."

Just then the brother arrived. "There's no sign of Dr. Windberg," he said. He held up a phone. "This is his."

Nahim frowned. "Why is Windberg separated from his phone? Has he been attacked?" He turned his accusing glare to Jax.

Jax shook his head. "Not by us. I'd like to have a talk with him myself, for attacking Abby over five years ago and for attacking me today. I'm quite happy to bring him in here, where we can sort this out."

Nahim obviously agreed. He looked at his brother. "And?"

The brother took a deep breath. "I'm wondering if there isn't something to what she says," he said. "Windberg left behind the phone, and we have no other way to track him."

"What about the hotel that you booked for him?"

"He never checked in," his brother said sadly. "I'm afraid he's disappeared."

"But did he disappear by choice or has one of my enemies taken him out?" Nahim snapped, his voice turning ugly. He turned his gaze to Jax and Abby. "You need to find him."

Jax pulled out his phone and quickly sent Beau a message. When his phone rang a few minutes afterward, it was Griffin.

"We're running cameras inside the hospital and on all the nearby streets. We haven't seen Windberg leave the hospital yet."

Jax faced Nahim. "According to the video cameras, Windberg hasn't left the hospital yet."

"Then he is here." He turned to his brother. "Find him. If he's the one who did this to Abdul …"

The brother gripped Nahim's shoulder and said, "I'll find him."

"You might want to leave him alive long enough that we can get some answers to our questions," Jax said.

The brother shot him a look and said, "I'll consider it." And he disappeared.

"You're not leaving too, are you?" she asked Jax.

He smiled. "My job is to look after you. So, no, I'm not leaving you."

"You should be looking after my son."

"No," she rounded on the father. "*You* should be looking after your son." And, on that, she stepped up and glared at him. "Before somebody around you uses your son as a toy or a tool yet again for their own purposes."

He glared at her, then spun on his heels and returned to his son's bedside.

Jax looked at her. "I think you're redefining women for him."

"No," she said gently. "Just reaffirming that he prefers women from his country. They don't talk back."

He laughed, pulled her into his arms, and hugged her.

CHAPTER 16

ABBY HATED TO say it, but, with everything now at a standstill for the moment, her energy was dropping again. She walked toward Jax. "Any chance of going to the hotel for a break?"

He looked at her in surprise. "The hotel?"

"If Benjamin's here, I'm probably better off not to be," she said drily.

He checked his watch. "It's not quite seven. Sunset shouldn't be until nine tonight. Let me check." He pulled out his phone and quickly called Griffin, telling him what they were doing.

"It's not a bad idea at that," Griffin said. She could hear his voice through the phone. "She probably needs to lie down."

"Yes," Abby said. "And I'd just like to know that I'm safe for a few minutes."

"Then why not take a few hours?" Griffin asked. "At least until we locate Benjamin."

"You got security covered at the hotel?" Jax asked Griffin.

"We will," he said. "Just take it easy. Go slow and careful."

"Always," Jax said. And, with that, he led her through the hospital and outside to the hotel. Even the fresh air perked her up. As they walked on the street, everybody around them was oblivious to the stress of the nightmare they were currently living.

She said, "It's so weird to be involved in this, when the world around us is ignorant. They are living a life without knowing how dark the underbelly is."

"I know," he said. "It's something I deal with all the time." He turned, glanced behind him, and urged her on a little faster.

She looked at him. "Is there a reason why we're almost running?"

"Yes," he said. "I think we're being followed."

Instantly she turned.

"Don't look now," he muttered. He wrapped an arm around her and tilted his head so it rested against hers. "Let the world think we're lovers."

"If that's what it takes," she agreed. "Do you think it's Benjamin?"

"I'm not sure if we have another element here to worry about."

"Could be MI6 keeping an eye on us?"

"Then they suck at their job," he said bluntly.

She chuckled at that and then gasped. "How can I find anything funny in all this?"

"Better to find something funny than to cry."

"Do you see how close to tears I am?" she asked. "It's not what I wanted at all."

"Doesn't matter if you want to or not," he said. "Sometimes it overtakes us."

"Maybe it's dealing with Abdul that hurts so much. That little boy's been through all of this over what?"

"You really think somebody tried to kill him?"

"We all know that," she said steadily. "The father continues to deny the options of who had access."

"Oh, his brain is working. He knows that he doesn't have very many people in that inner circle of his. And I think, as much as he might not want to believe it, your word does have weight. The fact that you exonerated his wife and her mother …"

"And I sure as hell hope that I'm right in doing so," she said. "We've seen cases where mothers and grandmothers killed family members without a thought, but, in this case, it's not like either the mother or the grandmother are getting attention from Abdul's near death. And the mother is pregnant yet again."

"Well, I, for one, agree with you," he said. "And the most likely suspect is Benjamin. We've had him pigeonholed as the bad guy right from the beginning."

"And I wonder if that's made us careless," she muttered. She stopped abruptly. She didn't recognize the area. "Where are we?"

"Going somewhere safe," he said cheerfully.

And, just like that, he steered her into an alleyway that didn't lead anywhere familiar. And then they were at a door, which opened in front of them. He quickly nudged her inside, and she found herself in the back stairwell of some hotel. She looked around, then at him. "Dodgy much? Are we renting by the hour?"

He chuckled and urged her up the stairs. "We're going to the third floor, so let's move along."

"Is that safe?"

"This is as safe as we'll get right now."

When they reached the third floor, a big steel door faced her. She raised an eyebrow. He tapped on the door, but it was an odd knock. The door open, and the woman on the other side looked at them both, but her gaze was hard and knowing. Her face was lean, as if she'd spent way too many years without food. But Abby revised her opinion. This woman was in fighting form, to the extent that Abby herself had never seen before. The stranger let them in and then said, "Straight down the hallway to the left."

Following instructions blindly and wondering why and what instinct within humanity drove her and others to do that, Abby went into the designated room. Sure enough, it was a bedroom.

As they stepped in, Jax said, "Hang on."

She stopped as he quickly searched the entire room. She looked at him and asked, "Even here?"

"Even here," he nodded. He went to the door, shut it, and locked it. "Now, my dear, you have a bed."

She looked at it with longing but first walked over to the window and went to throw the curtains wide open, but Jax stopped her.

"No."

She groaned, nodded, kicked off her shoes, walked back to the bed, and fell down face-first. Only as her head hit the pillow did she realize just how damn tired she truly was. She snuggled deeper into the pillows, murmuring, "I'm so done."

A blanket landed lightly on her shoulders.

"Don't you need to sleep?" she muttered.

"I will in a bit," he said.

"Do we only have four hours?"

"Maybe," he said. "Maybe less."

"Such a waste," she said with a big yawn.

"In what way?" he asked, but his voice was distracted.

"Because any other time that I've been sequestered in a

room with a badass, sexy, and available male," she said with yet another yawn, "I'd have found something better to do than sleep." And, on that note, she dropped into a deep slumber.

⚓

JAX STARED AT her in shock. Not only had she uttered words that he would love to act upon but she'd fallen asleep as if somebody had pulled the plug on her. It was amazing. He'd worked hard to get a similar ability, but then, as a doctor, she was probably forever being called out or had to deal with many scenarios where sleep was something she grabbed at any chance. Still, it was a skill he admired. He crashed softly on the bed beside her, reached over, and tucked her up close. He was gratified when she cuddled closer. He thought he heard a murmur. He leaned closer and asked, "What did you say?"

"Took you long enough," she muttered. And then her breathing returned to deep and even breaths.

He chuckled and said, "Didn't know you cared."

But, of course, he did. The signs were all there. Everything between the two of them had been leading up to them having so much more. Yet, at the same time, the circumstances were definitely not cooperating. He closed his eyes but kept opening them up at regular intervals. Another habit he'd trained himself to do, always checking to make sure they remained safe. He slept in a light REM sleep, grabbing ten minutes at a shot. By the time she murmured and rolled onto her back, her eyes opening, he felt like he'd grabbed at least two hours. But he knew it wasn't enough. Still, it would power him up for another bout of whatever was to come.

She smiled up at him, looped her arm around his neck, and came in close. "I don't know how long I was out," she said, "but it doesn't feel like it was very long."

"A couple hours, maybe a bit longer," he said, murmuring.

"Did you manage to close your eyes?"

He nodded. "A little bit." His phone buzzed again. He checked it. "Still no sign of Benjamin."

"Are we safe here?"

He nodded. "If nothing else, Benjamin doesn't have the firepower or the skills to break the defenses here."

"What is this, an MI6 safehouse?"

He didn't answer.

She leaned up on an elbow and stared at him in shock. "Seriously?"

He gave her a glimmer of a smile and asked, "How about you just don't ask questions?"

"Good deal," she said, collapsing back down. "There's just something about being free from all that, at least for a moment."

"It's very important."

She yawned again. "Must we go back so soon?"

"No. I don't see any point in leaving until they've got Benjamin. Do you?"

She shuddered. "I would just as soon not go back even when they do have him. There's no reason for me to be involved at all at this point."

He leaned over and kissed her gently on the temple. "Well, you were a major part of this right from the beginning, so you may want to see it through to the end, if only to put the nightmares to rest."

"Only if that means Benjamin's dead," she muttered.

"And I know that's a terrible thing to say, but he's a terrible man."

"And yet, we haven't seen him, not really," Jax said thoughtfully. "That's always bothered me."

"What?"

"That he's a ghost. I didn't see him. You haven't seen him. And, although the MI6 security team thinks they saw him once in a doctor's lab coat, that photo was a little bit indistinct for me."

"Meaning, you think it might not have been him?" she cried out. She sat up in bed, looked down at him. "If there's one thing you must understand, that *is* Benjamin. He was always this ghost in the hallways during med school. He'd be in class, and you'd turn around, and he'd be gone again. He was one of those people who everybody loved to ignore and to overlook. And it sounds like he's still doing the same thing in his career and his personal life."

"We've all met people like that," he said. "I remember in school, one mother complained because her son never made it into the yearbook, and she was astonished when people barely even recognized his name. He'd been one of those who, although he'd attended class, he was always in the background. He walked the hallways, and nobody ever really knew him. It was pretty disconcerting for the mother to hear that, and then, when we heard, for us to realize how much we hadn't even seen him either."

"Well, Benjamin was like that. But that also made it even creepier when I found out he was following me everywhere."

"Do you think he still is?"

She dropped down on her back again. "Well, if he is, that would mean he'd know exactly where we are now.

Because, if there's one thing he was really good at, it was stalking someone."

"So maybe he does know," Jax said thoughtfully. "It'd be interesting if he entered this building."

"Why?"

"Because plenty of cameras are here, and DeeDee will be watching them."

"DeeDee?"

"The woman outside."

"That woman who looks like she'd rather slice open your throat than let you have a cup of coffee is called DeeDee?"

He flashed a grin.

She chuckled. "Oh, my goodness," she said. "Talk about misnaming someone."

"I think she has a more complex and Far East–sounding name, but DeeDee is the shortened version."

She laid on her back, smiling at the ceiling. "Thank you. I needed that. Just something lighthearted to remind me that there's so much more in the world than Benjamin."

"He's been a threat over your shoulder for a long time, hasn't he?"

She nodded. "The trouble is, he's always been that big boogeyman. I just didn't know it at first. I thought he wasn't anything to be afraid of until he caught me. It didn't take long for him to completely disable me to the point that I almost didn't get free. If the neighbors hadn't heard me screaming, I have no doubt that he would have imprisoned me in my house for however long he chose to and would do any number of unspeakable things to me also because he chose to."

"Sounds like he has no care for anybody else, like a true sociopath."

"Exactly. It's amazing just how much he's impacted my life, leaving that heaviness in the background. Even after he was gone, he wasn't ever really gone."

"Well, after this," Jax said, "he'll be gone."

"Promise?"

He looked at her gently and nodded. "I promise."

She reached her arms around him, leaned up, and kissed him. "Good. Now isn't there something better for two people on a bed to do than talk?"

"Absolutely," he murmured and lowered his head.

CHAPTER 17

ABBY CHUCKLED AS his lips met hers. "I figured you might have some ideas." And she kissed him as she'd been wanting to since the first time she'd faced him, standing before her, fully geared up and looking so damn dangerous. Only to find out he was a softy on the inside. But an honorable softy. And the whole package was irresistible. At least for her. Even as he chuckled, the warm breath from his mouth mixed and mingled with hers as their lips gently stroked back and forth, tongues tasting and testing, lips soft and gentle as the pressure and the tension slowly eased, knowing that this is where they were and that this is what they were about—and not only that but that they both wanted it. He lifted his head for a moment, and she looked up at him and said, "Don't even think to question me."

His lips quirked, and his head came back down. He gave her a kiss that seemed to force a response from deep inside her. She'd fully intended to respond with all her heart, but it seemed like he was after her soul too. And she had no recourse but to give it to him, her body melting against his in compliance and in complete agreement as his heated kiss drove through her, comingling with his soul, as if he could see right through her head to her toes. When he finally lifted his head, she gasped and said, "Wow, that's deadly."

"Good," he said, a tremor in his voice. "Because that was

my exact response too. You pack a hell of a powerful punch, lady." And then he lowered his head again.

She wrapped her arms around his neck and held on tight. She wanted this, and she wanted so much more, but she'd take this for the moment. He was something to be experienced, even if she had to walk away afterward with her tail between her legs, yet her head held high. She still wanted every moment she could have with him.

When he lifted his head the next time though, she followed his head up and claimed his lips for her own, kissing him back with all the power and presence that she had available and letting him know exactly how much she wanted him right now. He rolled over, giving her the lead, and she sat up, straddling his hips, pulling her shirt over her head, then tossing it to the side as he reached up and unclipped her bra.

As soon as the soft pink cups fell away, his breath caught in the back of his throat as he stared in awe.

"It's always nice to see a reaction like that," she teased.

He cupped her breasts gently, holding the weight of them in his hands. He shook his head and whispered, "Gorgeous." Then he sat up with her still straddling his hips, wrapping his arms around her and holding her close.

She pushed him back gently and said, "You're wearing too many clothes." With her help, they quickly stripped off his shirt, and he hugged her tight. Skin against skin, heat against heat, she moaned softly as her breasts flattened against his chest. She just laid against him for a long moment, loving the feel of togetherness. "It's been a long time for me," she admitted.

He held her tight and whispered, "For me too."

She smiled at that. She didn't know if he was lying or

not, but she appreciated the thought. "A big beautiful guy like you?" she asked, shaking her head. "I doubt it."

"A smart beautiful lady like you?" he asked, shaking his head too. "I doubt it too."

She burst out laughing and stood while he lay there, watching her. She stepped back and shucked out of her jeans, leaving just a scrap of pink lace in play, with her socks on as well. She motioned at him. "Your turn." He hopped off the bed and quickly stripped off everything, his masculinity erect and ready, standing proudly in front of her. She smiled and walked over to the edge of the bed and said, "You get to take this piece off."

He reached out gently and slipped his fingers under the elastic and drew the thong down to her ankles, where she stepped out of them. But his eyes never left the tiny triangle of hair at her privates.

He gave a happy sigh. "You are seriously beautiful." His gaze wandered from her knees to her hips to her ribs to her breasts to her shoulders. "Everything is perfectly aligned. It's like God did all the rest of His practice, and then, when He got to you, He finally made the real thing."

She was touched. "I think that's the nicest thing anybody has ever said to me. Of course it's absolute garbage, but hey."

He grinned, looked at her, and said, "I'm not so sure it is. You're very blessed in the genetics of biology."

"I am," she said. "And so are you." She dragged him to the bed with her, and she wrapped her arms around his neck, the two of them locking gazes as she whispered, "Now you can kiss me."

"Isn't that what we have been doing?" he asked as he drifted kisses down her neck, making her moan as the goose bumps raised up and down her skin, her shoulders, and all along her back. When his hand slid up to her ribs, just resting below her breasts, she shifted, wanting his hands on her more. But he refused. His lips shifted from side to side, gently caressing her skin, tasting and teasing.

She drew her hands through his hair, stroking, holding him close and loving the feel of togetherness at the moment. She desperately wanted this time with him. She worried a call would come through to interrupt them, not wanting the reminder that neither had turned off their cell phones. No way they could. Not given the situation. But she refused to think about that right now.

She shifted, caught his head in her hands, and kissed him gently with all the fierce longing she'd held deep inside. She pulled him with her as she then rolled over, so she sat astride him, a move that happened so fast that he stared at her in shock. She chuckled and said, "My turn."

And she gently explored his body, her fingers stroking across the ribs, the plains, the hollows, the muscles, and the scars. She kissed the edge of one scar and didn't even bother to ask where it came from. The man was a warrior, and his body was a testament to his survival skills. She took his nipple and grazed her teeth across the edge, fingers raking across the other one.

He shifted, his manhood hard and powerful beneath her.

She gently slid down lower and lower, her hand stroking and caressing until she could grasp him fully in her hand. She stroked once, twice, and leaned over and gently slipped her tongue along the top of it. He groaned, his hips rising and asking for so much more. But she held him steady, her fingers caressing until she cupped the two globes beneath and gently squeezed them.

He groaned and said, "No more of that."

But she didn't listen to him. Instead her mouth gently came down over the top, her lips sealed tight as she stroked him with her tongue, teasing him and caressing him. And just when she was about to take more of him deeper into her throat, he picked her up, tossed her down, and flipped until he was on top. And he growled, "My turn."

And when he slid down, he slid all the way down, his mouth coming down on top of her most intimate place. The gasps escaped her lips as her hips heaved upward. He held her firm in his hands as he tasted her deeply, taking each of the outer lips and sucking them deep into his mouth.

She twisted underneath him. "No, no, no," she said. "Come to me." But he was merciless until her body exploded as the climax ripped through her with a ferocity that she had never felt before.

Then he rose up before her, grabbed her hips, and seated himself deep into the heart of her.

She laid trembling in shock as the orgasm still worked through her.

When he started to move, she didn't even have a chance to catch her breath. A second climax climbed up her throat, ready to explode. She held back ever-so-slightly, but he was having none of it.

"Relax," he said. "Let it come." As he said that, his fingers gently massaged the nub between her legs. That second orgasm ripped through her. She cried out, but he didn't stop even then. Not until he plowed deep time and time again, raising the tempo and shifting her position until she was once again screaming underneath him.

And this time, she cried out, "I want you with me."

He leaned over, and his pace picked up until he dove into her faster and faster and faster, and suddenly he groaned, his body shaking uncontrollably as he poured himself into her.

And set off yet another orgasm in Abby. She laid trembling in his arms as he collapsed beside her, tucking her up close. She'd known it would be heaven, but she hadn't realized it would be … *this*. And, even now, as she laid on his chest, still gasping for air, she knew nothing she'd ever experienced came close to *this*.

He pulled her up tight against him. "You okay?"

She nodded. "Better than okay," she gasped. "Never better."

"Good," he whispered. "I didn't want you to forget me."

She groaned and whispered, "I don't want you to forget me either. Feels like we're two ships in the night, but it's going to be dawn soon, and I'm trying to figure out how to make it night again so we can meet up for a second time." Just as she said that, he rolled her slightly forward onto her belly and slid inside her from behind. She groaned as he slowly and gently stroked deeper inside, his fingers raising her torment from the front as he loved her again over and over and over. By the time they had shared a fourth orgasm, and he collapsed back down, she was mindless jelly. "My God," she murmured. "I wasn't expecting that."

"Well, like I said, it's been a long time."

She was too tired to even giggle. She just held him close, her body completely filled with emotions and energy and humming with music she hadn't heard ever before. "Is it okay if I nod off to sleep again?"

"Sleep," he whispered. "We must catch it while we can."

"Still think it's a waste," she murmured.

His hand slipped between her legs as he teased the soft folds, and she groaned. "We can keep going if you want," he murmured, his voice warm against her ear. He stroked her once, twice, and she could feel faint tremors roaming through her again.

"How is that possible?" she asked with a sigh.

"Sometimes it happens that way." And he pulled her closer. "To be continued later. Sleep now."

She sighed, her body completely sated. Then she closed her eyes and fell asleep.

⚓

JAX LAY HERE, cuddling Abby. His body completely depleted, yet still wanting more. When one tasted heaven, there would never be anything quite like it ever again. And, boy, was she the sweetest thing. But this wasn't just a physical attraction, and that's the part that worried him. He really liked her and wanted to get to know her more, spend time with her—hell, spend every damn night possible with her. But how would he do that? He thought back to his arrangement as the Mavericks team lead on this op. He had said *one job*, and this was his one job. But then what? It seemed like, once with the Mavericks, they were all on call.

Which wasn't bad. Especially since they could accept or reject each op as it came. Or at least Jax hoped so.

He couldn't believe that Griffin had found a woman, and now Jax had too. He hadn't believed it at the time, but now he needed to figure out just what he would do for a job and a career—to make something of his life—so that Abby wouldn't mind being with him. He didn't think she'd like him doing these jobs, but maybe she'd understand after seeing just how important her rescue had been. He shelved all thoughts of the future for the moment, closed his eyes, and tried to let his body rest.

When a text came through, he reached for his phone and checked it. A text from Griffin.

They got him.

Jax smiled, dropped the phone beside him, and whispered, "They got him." He felt her stir.

"They caught Benjamin?"

"Yes," he whispered.

She rolled onto her back and opened her eyes. "Does that mean we get to stay here?"

Just then his phone rang. "I highly doubt it," he said with a shake of his head. But he leaned over, his body already awakening at the sight of her slumberous eyes. And he slid gently inside her, even as he answered the phone. With one hand, he held her tethered close, and, with his other, he held the phone and asked, "What's up?"

"We need you back at the hospital," Beau said. "Security found him."

"Where was he?"

"Hiding in the laundry room in the hospital basement," he said. "And he's telling a very different tale."

"Oh?"

"Yeah," Beau said. "Both of you get over here fast."

"On the way," he said. He dropped the phone, leaned over, kissed her hard, and pressed his hips against her several times before his own orgasm ripped through him and helped her to climb over the edge once again. And then, as he lay here, trying to breathe, he murmured, "Now we must go."

She groaned and said, "That's a hell of a way to wake up."

"It is, isn't it?" he said with a chuckle. He leaned over, kissed her hard, and smacked her gently on the bum. "Now." He got up and headed to the bathroom.

CHAPTER 18

B ACK AT THE hospital, Abby looked at Jax and asked, "They'll know, won't they?"

He laughed. "Well, we do look a little too alert to have slept the whole time."

She smiled and linked her fingers with his. As they walked into the front entrance to the hospital, security met up with them. "Was security behind us the whole way?"

He laughed. "I guess you didn't see them this time since it's dark now."

Beau met them at the doorway and told Jax, "I need you to come with me." Then he turned to Abby and said, "You have the choice of looking in on Abdul, being with Danny and the boy's family, or coming with us."

She hesitated, but Jax made the decision for her. "Let's get you somewhere you can stay comfortably." And they quickly diverted her to the sitting room where the rest of the family was. Two of the family's security guards were here as well. "I'll send over a couple MI6 agents as well."

As soon as she was settled, Jax headed off with Beau. She frowned as they disappeared. She didn't like being separated from him at all and, even worse, it sounded like they had had Benjamin, but they'd lost him. She sat down, and the father looked at her.

"They found him. But they won't let me speak with

him."

"Understood," she said. She pulled out her phone and quickly sent a message to Jax. **Something's going on,** she texted. **What?**

Benjamin's possibly dead.

She gasped as she stared down at the message. **Call me.**

Can't. We'll talk in a few minutes.

She put away her phone and sat, studying the father's angry face. He kept staring out the window and then back at his wife and then out the window. While Nahim was obviously upset, the wife appeared to be at peace and had curled up on the corner of a couch with her eyes closed. Her belly was cradled in her hands. She had already given birth to five daughters, one son, and now was on her seventh child. The marvel of a woman's body continuously amazed Abby. As she sat here, she heard a commotion outside. One of the guards stepped out, and the other one stood at attention, waiting for something to happen.

She frowned, got up, walked over to him, and asked, "Do you know what's going on?"

He shook his head but turned as the door opened. The second guard stepped in, stood at the doorway, looked at her, and said, "You're needed outside." Then he stepped backward.

Something about the awkward stiffness to his movements made her worry.

She was called again. "Please come."

Hesitatingly and with an odd look at the guard now frowning at the door, she said, "I don't like the sound of this."

"Neither do I." He stepped in front of her and went through the double doors. There was a hard spit, and the guard ahead of her collapsed to his knees and fell onto the floor. She was already half out. Her hand was grabbed, and she was dragged all the way out.

"What's going on?" she cried out. The other guard, his face pale, stood off to the side. Behind him was Benjamin. She stared at him in shock. "They said you were dead."

"No," he said. "But I did find a reasonably good facsimile of someone who looks like me. And he's wearing my ID."

"That makes sense," she muttered. "You're too mean to die."

He smiled at her warmly. "Nonsense," he said. "I was never mean to you. At least not when you were nice to me. You're the one who insists on causing me trouble." Then he looked at the other soldier and said, "Go help your friend."

Immediately the soldier walked over and bent to check on his friend's condition. When a second hard spit came, he keeled over on top of the first body.

She held her hands to her lips. "You didn't have to kill him," she cried out.

"No," he said. "I didn't. But it's a very freeing experience. You should try it sometime."

"Killing people?" she asked in shock.

"Yes. You don't always have to be such a Pollyanna and save people, you know?"

"Well, I much prefer that," she snapped. "We're not all sociopaths like you."

"If you're trying to make me feel better," he said, grinning, "that's a good way to do it. I went to a lot of effort to get you back in my grasp again. It's not like I'll let you get away with anything now." He dragged her down the hallway toward the other set of double doors.

"And does Nahim know what you did?"

"I don't give a shit if he does or not," Benjamin said. "My time was up there anyway. I raked in as much money as I could off all the family members, and then I planned to leave. You were my ticket out of there at the same time."

"And you would just kill that little boy?"

"Little boy, little girl, man, woman, why would I care?"

She took a deep breath, realizing just how unfeeling and unconcerned he was about causing such deaths. She glanced back at the double doors to see Nahim's head poking out, and the look on his face.

"Benjamin," he yelled.

Benjamin lifted his handgun and fired in the direction of the father. And then he shoved her out the door roughly. "Damn it. I didn't want him to see us." He pushed her through to a set of stairs. "Let's go. Fast, fast, fast."

"You know Nahim will come after you," she said. "You tried to kill his son."

"But did I?" he asked. "He doesn't have a clue who his enemies truly are."

"Meaning that his brother was in on it too?"

"Do you really think his brother would have mounted a big attack like that on the cruise ship just for me?"

"So why did he then?"

"Money," Benjamin said, laughing. "I made a huge haul from Nahim. Even the mother paid me to look after Abdul so well. The uncles paid me too. Everybody paid me, for various reasons. I took all that money and more. And I paid off the brother to help me get you under the guise that I needed you for the boy, but I made sure I gave Abdul an extra shot of arsenic so that there would be maximum pain on my way out the door."

"That makes no sense," she whispered. "How can you be

such a monster?"

"Easy," he said, laughing. "You must pick and choose what's important in life."

"I'm not important," she cried out.

"I know that," he said. "Once I determined that you weren't worthy, I realized that I had the power to do something that I wanted to do for a long time."

"And what's that?" she asked, hating to even hear the answer because she knew it would make her sick to her stomach. He wasn't just a monster but he was a sick individual, one of those who cared nothing about the pain he caused and probably enjoyed it all too much.

"I will make you pay," he said. "I have a place all picked out for us."

"And what if I don't want to go?"

"Who said I would ask you? You'll do what I say because otherwise I'll come back and kill everybody else in here. For all you know, I've left bombs everywhere. You know how I operate. I really don't give a shit about anyone."

She thought about the cruise liner and his lack of care for anyone's life. "What about Bahan?"

"That's who I planned to leave on the floor in the hospital laundry room. But you guys had already met him, so that didn't go to plan. He was supposed to keep himself away from detection."

"It doesn't always work though, does it?" she asked. "Plans are meant to be changed."

"Well, if I change mine, that means killing you. Now hurry up," he snapped, and he pushed her forward down the stairs. She held on to the railing to stop herself from falling all the way down the stairs. She ran down ahead to the landing, hoping that Nahim was at least contacting somebody and letting them know what had happened. But then maybe Nahim hated her so much, enough to let her go with Benjamin. She didn't know.

"And what about Nahim's brother, Bahan? Did you kill him yet?"

"Well, he's on the run himself."

"Why?" she asked.

"Because the two of us were most likely the ones who had administered the arsenic to the little boy."

"It *was* you," she said. "So what did Bahan do?"

"He administered most of it. I just finished it."

"You were both feeding the little boy poison?"

"Sure. Not enough to do any harm though. But you know what it's like. Cumulative."

"It's deadly," she snapped. "And why did the child's uncle do it?"

"Because he didn't know Nahim's wife was pregnant, and, of course, the father's got a target on his back. He has for a long time. He's made a lot of changes within his little fiefdom," he said caustically. "And nobody's happy about it. The brother would take over. He's got four sons and would be much harder to usurp."

"A bullet would kill him too," she snapped. "My God. You people are living on a completely different planet."

"Not really," he said. "We're just living life the way we want to, unlike you, who spends your life living for other people. I'm living for myself." He pushed through another set of double doors and down more stairs. She had no idea where he was taking her. Presumably somewhere alone so that he could secret her away.

"What are your plans now?" she asked.

"You'll find out. I didn't spend years planning this to

just let you get away from me here now. Do you think I'm stupid?"

"Of course not," she said. "You've always been a threat to my life."

"Damn right," he snapped. "Make sure you remember it."

She didn't understand the mentality, but then she'd seen a lot of broken minds in her lifetime, even just through the courses she'd taken. She tried to remember the psychology of dealing with a sociopath, but basically it was to remember they didn't give a shit about anything or anyone but their own pleasure. And that didn't bode well for Abby. "Did you kill anybody else?"

"No, not really. Why?" he answered.

She frowned at that. "*Not really?*" She paused. "Meaning, that you only participated somewhat in their deaths or that you didn't quite kill them or that you have no clue?"

He laughed. "What's the matter? Did you miss me? Want to know all the details of my life since we were together?"

"It's been over five years, and we were never together," she said. "I have wondered how much trouble you've gotten into in that time."

"None," he said. "Surprise, surprise. Only you. You're the one stopping me from going back home again."

"Because of the court case?"

"Of course, because of the court case," he snapped. "You're not that stupid."

"No," she said. "Neither of us are. We made it through med school and that means we have a certain amount of smarts."

"But you're a Goody Two-shoes, whereas I look after

just me. I'm the only one who counts."

"Well, I care about other people," she said.

He nodded. "Maybe, but that has nothing to do with this right now. You're the one stopping me from returning to the US. I can't get that case squashed. I'm on this bloody wanted list for having skipped the country, and I had to stay in a country without extradition. I've been going from private practice to private practice, but I want my life back," he said. "So you'll drop all charges, and then you'll quietly disappear, so they can't come after me again."

"But I can't drop the charges." The blow came out of nowhere, smacking her hard enough on the head that she fell to her hands and knees. Gasping desperately and trying to get her brain to stop rattling around inside her skull and seeing only black and white spots in her eyes, she was then grabbed roughly by the upper arm and dragged to her feet again.

"Yes, you can," he said, his voice dead. "Or else I'll put a bullet in you right now."

She took several deep breaths. "Fine. I will."

"See? It really doesn't take anything to get what you want in life," he said. "Everybody is quite happy to do what I want them to do."

"What I meant to say," she said, moving carefully, her head still pounding and her vision still not quite back to normal, "is that, even if I do drop the charges, that doesn't mean that they will."

"Sure, they will," he said. "Particularly if you're not around for them to worry about anymore. Without a victim, there's no case."

"You mean, for those kinds of charges. And you don't expect to face any charges for killing me. Is that it?"

"That's it," he said cheerfully. "And nobody over here gives a shit what happens to you. You're just a number, another pain in the ass by making it all happen in England. You should have just come to Dubai."

"And you should have just had me picked up quietly somewhere," she snapped. "Instead of getting your bloody henchmen to kill those people."

"We decided that was the way to do it right off the bat. How were we to know so many idiotic people would be there, and nobody would even know who you were?"

"Or that I would hear the commotion and disappear on the ship," she said.

"Yes. It wasn't even one of the megacruises. It was a small one, but still just so many people there."

"Were you on board?" she asked, staring at him in shock.

He laughed. "No, I wish. Life's kind of boring, but, if you can orchestrate shit like that every once in a while, it makes it more fun. You've got to make things lively."

"By poisoning a child, taking over a cruise ship, and making everybody believe that I'm necessary?"

He nodded. "It all makes sense."

"You're insane. *None* of this makes sense," she cried out. "Did Nahim know about the cruise ship plan?"

"Nope. We gave him only a brief overview. He didn't take part in any of it, but now he'll be blamed. It all makes sense if you realize the bottom line was I wanted you. That's it. I didn't care how we did it. But, once I told Bahan that you were on the cruise, it was supposed to be a subtle operation. Go snag you, take you away on a day trip, and bring you back to Dubai. But, no, he wanted more control. He wanted to be the big chief, controlling fire-and-ice stuff.

He did hire the wrong men too. So it ended with me hiring the wrong person, him hiring the wrong crew, and I don't know where the hell that guy helping you out came from, but that just made things worse."

"Jax?"

"Whatever," he said. "And who the hell has a name like that?" He waved his free hand. "Regardless, the pirates had big plans. But theirs weren't Bahan's plans. Still, it's funny that he's the one who escaped."

"So Bahan is Abdul's uncle?"

"Yeah. He is Nahim's head of security. Bahan went over on his own time, rigged this up, and was planning to leave everything with the pirates, so he wouldn't have to pay them and could just take you off the ship."

"Well, that makes more sense than what I've heard so far," she said. "You do know that more than twenty pirates died on that cruise ship, right?"

He whistled. "Wow. Bahan didn't say anything about that."

"Of course not," she said, "because that would expose his failure. Jax and his friend took them all out."

He stopped, turned her around, and stared at her. "Two men took out twenty-plus armed men?"

She nodded. "Bahan didn't do anything but come running home with my message."

Benjamin's face darkened with anger. "What a lying piece of shit. That's not what he said."

"Of course it isn't," she said. "You know perfectly well that these guys won't tell you the truth."

"Well, they aren't supposed to lie to me," he snapped.

"But didn't you lie to them?"

He stared at her. "And none of that has anything to do

with you."

She laughed. "It's ridiculous, all of it," she said. "Because, of course, they lied to you, and you lied to them. That's how you guys operate, isn't it?"

"Maybe," he said, "but who cares? Bahan won't live anyway. Not sure Nahim will either."

"So who will take Nahim's place?"

"Not my problem," he said. "I really don't care."

"If you say so," she said. "But you could try living peaceful for once."

"When I'm dead," he said. "But, for now, I'll disappear again to live long and happy."

"Just not in the US."

At that, her shoulder was squeezed really hard. She cried out in pain, but he didn't let go. He shoved his head against hers and said, "Yes, in the US, you bitch. You'll fix what you did. I didn't have anything to do with that. You know you wanted me in your house, and you're the one who invited me in."

She could barely even hear his words from the pain slamming through her body. She knew he was trying to dislocate her shoulder. He'd succeed too. She gasped several times, easing back the crippling pain so she could figure out what the hell she could do. Her mind raced, but it found nothing useful. "Stop," she yelled.

He released her shoulder just to shut her up and said, "And remember that, anytime you go against me, I'll just hurt you more."

A witty retort was on her tongue, but she held it back because it wasn't worth yet another painful blow or torturing grip. She looked around, seeing great big furnace pipes and other ductwork on the ceiling. "Where are we?"

"Down in the basement."

"And how do we get out?"

"The same way we got in," he said. "There are many ways in and out of a hospital. Remember that."

She thought about it and shrugged. "I guess an awful lot of exits and entrances exist just for the morgue and for the shipping requirements."

"Exactly," he said.

"And then what?"

"You'll go to my place," he said. "And you'll write out a very nice letter, dropping all the charges, stating how you feel terribly guilty for having accused me of any of these crimes."

"That might work," she admitted. It *would* probably work, and everybody would be happy to close the case and to forget about it.

"Of course it will. Do you really think anybody'll stop me?"

"Well, I was hoping one or two would," she said, sighing heavily.

"If you're talking about that macho male who hung close to you," he said, "I took him out easily enough."

"Was that you?"

"Well, somebody I paid. It was a bit of a joke. He was a buddy of mine, and he just clobbered him as he walked past. Never saw it coming."

"Of course not because he didn't realize that your buddy was a threat."

"Exactly. But you must realize threats come from all directions," he said. "And that's what I specialize in."

It's exactly what he specialized in, and it drove her crazy. Down in the bowels of the basement, he led her through the laundry room and out to the other side. "Remember. If we see anybody," he said, "you're not to say anything because I'll put a bullet in your head as soon as you do."

"But then you won't be allowed back into the US," she snapped.

"Sure, I will," he said. "I'll just fake your letter. Better to do it with your wording and with your handwriting, but, if I have to, I'll try it without." She winced and he laughed.

Up ahead were double doors, and she knew, as soon as they went through that and headed outside—into the dark night—chances of her ever getting free of Benjamin would be much less. In her head, she kept crying out for Jax. He had to be somewhere around. He had to have known that she was gone, and he had to be looking for her. But she didn't have a clue how to let him know.

"Now get ready," Benjamin said. "You better look like you love me and that you want to be with me and then anybody who asks gets a damn good and convincing story. Because not only will I kill you but I'll kill every person I see."

She bolted up a bright smile. "I understand perfectly. Let's go."

And he reached for the double doors.

⚓

JAX'S HEART SAT in his stomach like a great big rock that had no place to go. And it just kept festering in acids churning there. They'd already searched the hospital. Nahim had contacted him and the rest of the guards immediately. Once they found the two dead soldiers, everybody was on lockdown in the hospital. But it was a huge place, even with security assisting Jax as he desperately checked inside and outside. Griffin searched all the camera feeds, and still no sign of Benjamin was anywhere.

Once Jax realized that the body they'd found in the laundry room wasn't Benjamin's, then Jax knew Benjamin would go after Abby. Jax still raced through the entire hospital, finding no sign of her or Benjamin.

Just then he got a call from Griffin, saying, "Head down to the basement laundry room again. I think that's how Benjamin got in, and I'm pretty sure that's how he's heading out."

"Have you caught sight of him?"

"Not yet," he said in frustration. "That whole area has no cameras."

"That's ridiculous," Jax snapped. "This entire place should be completely covered with camera feeds."

"You and I both know that," Griffin said, "but nothing we say will make a difference here and now."

Groaning, Jax quickly raced to the stairs and headed down.

"At the next floor," Griffin continued, "change staircases and head to the service area."

It took another five valuable minutes to get where he needed to go. And finally he hit the same floor that the laundry room was on. He headed toward where they'd supposedly found Benjamin, but he wasn't here. Jax kept running and picked up the pace even more. "Still no sign of them?"

"No," Griffin said, "but we're narrowing it down. It'll be straight ahead of you, so watch your back."

With that, he hung up. Just then Beau contacted him.

"I'm coming up on the other side," he said. "I think we're about forty feet apart."

"And there's no sign of them," Jax said in frustration.

"No, but an exit is between us. I suggest we hit that exit fast and hard because they're likely to be just outside the door."

And there he was, at the double door. He pushed the door open as a bullet fired over his head. He slammed the door closed again. And then he opened it slightly. Suddenly Beau was right there with him. "We need eyes outside."

Beau pulled out his phone and snapped out orders. It wasn't a full minute before he had a report back. "Two people," he said. "Both of them in between the trucks parked in the delivery area, one of them a woman."

"Is it her?" Jax asked.

"Yes, it's her. He's holding a gun on her."

"Son of a bitch," Jax said.

"Move now," Beau said. "They're behind the trucks. We can get out of here without being shot at now."

They quickly bolted through the door, heading for the big trucks. Immediately Jax noted the streetlights in this parking area gave enough coverage for him to see Benjamin. And for Benjamin to see Jax and Beau. Jax headed to the concrete underneath and crawled his way forward. He could see legs up ahead. Beau was already on the other side of the truck, coming up from the far side, behind Benjamin and Abby. Just as Jax neared the front of the truck, Jax could hear Abby arguing.

"You can't just walk around with a gun in your hand. You know they'll shoot you."

"I don't give a shit," he said. "I'll make sure I shoot them first."

And, just like that, Jax was on the other side of the truck and pulled Benjamin's legs out from under him. Benjamin went down quickly but bounced back up, gun in hand, only to meet Jax's fists as Benjamin turned to face him. And then Jax couldn't stop pummeling Benjamin to the ground. Finally, in the distant recesses of his mind, he heard Abby crying out.

"Stop. Stop! He's down, unconscious. Leave him alone."

He shook his head. "I wanna make sure he stays down." Jax sat back slightly, and Beau approached with his handgun still gripped in his hand, looking down at Benjamin.

"Looks like we got him."

Jax nodded. "Yes, it's finally over."

"No, it's not," she said. "The uncle, the head of security, Bahan, we need to capture him. Benjamin here hired Bahan to do the cruise thing. Bahan then hired the pirates who took over the boat and the passengers. But you guys killed the pirates, and we let the uncle off. Nahim had no knowledge of all this."

"So it's not quite over," Jax said as he rolled Benjamin over and tied his hands behind him. "But Benjamin won't be kidnapping you again."

"Or giving little boys arsenic."

"So you were right?" Beau asked, looking at her.

Jax watched as she nodded.

"Yes and no. Both him and Bahan filled the boy with arsenic."

"What's wrong with these men?" Jax asked alongside an expletive.

"The uncle wanted to take over the family leadership," she said. "And Benjamin was just trying to create maximum chaos, which is what he likes to do. He was stealing money from the father but was also being paid by many family members, some to kill Abdul and some to keep the boy alive.

Benjamin took all the money paid to him. He was to pay the uncle for the cruise thing to collect me, and then, when the uncle didn't pay for the pirates because you guys killed them all, Benjamin didn't transfer the last of the money to the uncle either. So he's trying to disappear now with all the money, and he wants to return to the States, but I'm responsible for him not allowed to go back."

"You mean, as far as *he's* concerned, you're responsible," Jax said.

She smiled, gave him a quick nod, and said, "Exactly. But we must make sure that Bahan is picked up as well." She looked over to see Beau standing off to one side, dictating orders. "Do you guys just call up whoever you want and get whatever help you need?"

He gave her a slight grin and said, "Sounds like it. Works best that way." Then he reached over, tucked her up close, and hugged her. "Are you okay?"

She looked at Benjamin, still on the ground, just lying there, unconscious, and said, "Yes. I'd really like to kick him in the head myself, but there's seriously no point."

"No, there isn't. Whether MI6 gets ahold of him or not, he won't be out of jail for a long time." Benjamin seemed to come to, and Jax helped Benjamin to his feet as security men appeared, now checking out the area.

She told Jax, "Benjamin shot both guards waiting beside the boy where I was, so MI6 will very much want him."

"Good," he said. "I hope he rots a long way away from the US, and then at least he'll never make it home."

"I can't argue with that," she said.

Benjamin just glared at her. "Bitch, you know you'll never hold me anywhere."

"Probably," she said sadly. "But I hope the British jail

system is harder on you than anything the US could have thrown at you."

"I doubt it," he said as a bullet slammed into the truck trailer right beside them.

She cried out and, when another volley of bullets fired their way, she ducked behind Jax. He had already pulled Benjamin back, getting him out of the danger, but his sudden weight in Jax's arms told her everything. "He's been hit," she said as she dove to Benjamin, trying to save his life. But it was obviously too late. There was a bullet between his eyes. "Oh, my God," she said, staring at him.

"We must keep ourselves safe," Jax said. "I'm not sure who just did this."

"I'd say probably Bahan," she said. "It's the only thing that makes sense."

"Everybody else is on this too," Beau said. "We just need to keep it quiet."

Jax pulled her farther away and said, "Let's get you back inside." Beau nodded.

They left Benjamin where he was on the ground and raced to the end of the trailers, with Jax leading the way to open the door. They barreled inside the hospital and out of danger.

"I didn't hear any more shooting," she said.

"I suspect Bahan's gone," Jax said. "He got what he wanted."

"Only Benjamin can say anything about Bahan's involvement. Except for me."

"But Bahan might not know that," Jax said. "Let's get you back upstairs where you're under additional security."

"Why?" she asked sadly. "Those two young men lost their lives defending me." She looked up at Jax, tears in her eyes now. "So much death."

He nodded. "Unfortunately that's the battle we always face, day in and out."

She nodded. "If I ever forget why you do what you're doing, remind me of this, please." She smiled a brave smile, eyes shining with tears. "It'll make it much easier to keep letting you walk away."

He leaned over, kissed her head, and said, "It won't be that bad."

She nodded. "So you say."

Beau gave a hard laugh. "Glad to see you two finally got together."

"Well, we did," she said. "Just not long enough."

"You were only doing one mission, weren't you?" Beau asked, looking at Jax. "Or has that changed?"

He nodded. "But this one isn't quite done yet."

"True enough," Beau said. "It's easy to talk about the future afterward."

"You mean, when we're sure that we have a future?" Abby asked with spirit.

Beau nodded. "Exactly. Let's first make sure that Nahim and Abdul are safe because, with that uncle running around, Bahan still needs to take out the father and the son."

They raced to Abdul's bedside and, when they walked in, they found an eerie tableau facing them. The uncle was there, on the floor, somebody holding a gun on him. But not the somebody she had expected. Instead it was Abdul's mother. And she was trembling. Immediately Abby stepped forward, wrapped her arms around her, and said, "I know he deserves it. Both the doctor and Bahan here administered arsenic to your son."

The mother looked at her in tears, and she still pointed

the gun at Bahan, but her gun hand was shaking.

Jax stepped forward, pulled the gun from her hand, and said, "This isn't the way."

The mother sank down and cried. Abby hugged her while she checked to see how Abdul was doing, just as the boy woke up. She motioned for the mother to come to her son and said, "Look."

At that, the little boy's eyes widened, his gaze a whole lot clearer than it had been lately.

He smiled at his mum. "Mama?"

She let out a cry and wrapped her little boy up in her arms.

When Nahim arrived, he stepped forward to find his boy awake and looking so much better. He joined his wife and son on the bed. Only a few minutes later he turned to look at Abby and Jax holding a gun on his brother on the ground. Nahim frowned and asked, "What's the meaning of this?"

Jax quickly explained.

Nahim straightened, looked at his son, and then said to Bahan, "You would do this? You, who have four sons of your own, would kill my son when I have tried so hard?"

His brother sat up slowly and said, "You know how it is. I'm the eldest son. I was supposed to take Father's place."

"Yes, but our father gave it to me. You were not deemed worthy," he said. "And now I know why."

As Nahim neared his brother, Bahan pulled out a weapon of his own—but, instead of shooting Nahim, Bahan turned the gun on himself, shoved it under his jaw, and pulled the trigger.

CHAPTER 19

ABBY STARED AT the body on the ground and looked up at Jax and then at Beau.

Nahim stared at him and said, "This is a very difficult time for me."

"Obviously," she said. "Remember that part about not trusting those around you?"

"He was my brother."

"But he was ambitious," Beau said. "And that's always a death knell to friendships and families."

"Yes," Nahim said and turned to look at Abby. "And, even though Benjamin did it for all the wrong reasons, it's because of you that my son will now be okay."

"Well, me and Danny. And hopefully Abdul will fully recover," she said cautiously.

"Yes," Nahim said, looking at his son, tears of pride in his voice. "He's a fighter. He'll be just fine now."

"And in a very unconventional way," she said, "your son is being taken care of. And how sad that it had to happen in the first place," she said. "And you don't know all of it." She proceeded to explain what Benjamin had told her before he died.

His face pale, Nahim said quietly, "I hadn't realized, but I do know more now."

"And take it easy on your wife," she said in a hard tone.

"That woman has done nothing but be a good wife to you. You should treat her better. She's worn out. She's now pregnant for the seventh time and has her other six children to tend to, plus you."

He nodded. "I will look after her. Besides, she carries another son now."

Abby rolled her eyes at him. "Did you browbeat Danny into testing your wife?"

He smiled and said, "It does not matter. It's another boy. I know it."

"But, if it's a girl, you will not punish your wife or your new daughter."

"No," he said. "We'll just try again."

She sighed and had to be satisfied with that. As the father rejoined the mother and their son, Abby joined Jax and said, "You know what? As much as I hate this kind of an ending, it's not such a bad ending."

"Right. I was just thinking that," Jax said. "It's much better than court cases and trials and ugly recriminations and accusations and having to sort all the lies from the truth. The fact of the matter is, both bad guys are dead, and that is a blessing in disguise."

Just then the rest of the MI6 security team came inside, and, sure enough, there was Jonas. He looked at the dead man on the ground and asked, "When are you guys leaving again? You've overstayed your welcome," he growled. "Do you have any idea how much paperwork you've created?"

Beau laughed and said, "Come on. Let's talk."

Jax reached out a hand, and she placed hers in it.

"Where are we going?" she asked.

"Where do you want to go?" he said with a big smile. "It's a big bad world out there."

"It sure is," she said with a nod. "But I'd like to go wherever you're going."

"Oh, I thought that was my line," he said. "I'm the one who's basically done the mission I had planned on doing and just maybe can follow you around. You're the one with the job."

She chuckled. "But you'd be bored within a few days. I understand what you do now, so you do *you*, and I'll do *me* and, when we can, we'll be as close together as we can be."

He leaned over, gave her a hard kiss, and said, "I always plan on coming home, you know?"

"Well, if you do your best," she said, "I'll be good with that. I don't expect the world."

"Oh," he said, his eyes twinkling, "how about we go visit heaven again?"

She smiled, wrapped her arms around his neck, and whispered, "Now that's an idea I can get behind."

"For just once or twice?"

"How about forever? Heaven has no time frame."

"So true," he said, and he kissed her hard. "I can't stop kissing you. I don't think it's possible." And kissed her again.

She smiled inside, realizing that she had gained so much more from this trip than she'd never expected. When she finally pulled her head back, she said, "You know what? I need to thank a few people who insisted on me taking that damn cruise. In a very roundabout way, they've brought me exactly what I was looking for."

"And what was that?"

"An angel of my own," she whispered. "Just a very different type of heaven than I had envisioned. But much better." Then she laughingly kissed him lightly on his lips. "I'm so glad I found you."

"Ditto," he whispered and kissed her back.

EPILOGUE

BEAU MADISON WALKED along the New York City street until he came to the small coffee shop. He sat down, and coffee appeared magically in front of him. He smiled and picked up the cup and, underneath the saucer, was a number. He opened up his phone and quickly linked up the number to a website. There were instructions.

Good morning, Beau. Are you ready to go on your own mission?

Just then his phone rang. "Yes," he said. "Everybody said that we would do one job. What do you do when we run out of people?"

"It's hard to say," Jax said with a smile in his voice. "But I think we're moving into teams after this. Bigger teams for bigger jobs. And, for some of us, it's almost like a graduation party."

"So, once I've done this mission," Beau said, "I get to join you guys?"

"Yes," Jax said. "What we didn't realize was how this was an initiation. And I'm not allowed to tell you any more than that."

"Hey, I'm glad to even hear that much," he said, "because sometimes I think we're just disappearing into the middle of nowhere. Can't say I want to lose track of everyone."

"Right. But, if you're up for it, all details will be sent to you immediately."

"Sounds good," Beau said. And just before Jax signed off, Beau asked, "What's my destination?"

"You're heading up north. A cult's been picking up women and bringing them in as sex slaves."

"Shit," Beau said. "Some guys have all the luck."

"Well, maybe but maybe not," Jax said. "One of those women is the daughter of a very big business mogul. He runs a lot of high-couture modeling agencies. His daughter was picked up on her way from college, tossed into the back of the vehicle, and never seen again."

"How long ago?"

"Six days."

"Shit. So long ago? Why haven't we been called in earlier?"

"Nobody knew where she was. But they caught a potential sighting of her in Alaska about ten miles west of Anchorage just a couple of days ago."

"Well, Alaska is a good place to be at this time of year."

Jax laughed. "As long as you don't mind horseflies the size of mice."

"I remember those," Beau said with a groan. "Just me again?"

"Nope. An old buddy of yours is going too."

"Good. Who?"

"You'll see him when you arrive in Anchorage."

"And when the hell is that?"

"Tickets are already on your phone." And, with that, Jax hung up.

Beau checked the incoming slips to see he would fly out in exactly six hours. "Wow, you sure don't give a guy much time in between ops." Beau looked around and had enough time to finish his coffee and to eat something and then to grab some clean clothes before he was off on his own mission.

His own mission. That felt like a challenge for the first time in many years.

He was looking forward to it.

<blockquote>This concludes Book 3 of The Mavericks: Jax.
Read about Beau: The Mavericks, Book 4</blockquote>

The Mavericks: Beau (Book #4)

What happens when the very men—trained to make the hard decisions—come up against the rules and regulations that hold them back from doing what needs to be done? They either stay and work within the constraints given to them or they walk away. Only now, for a select few, they have another option:

The Mavericks. A covert black ops team that steps up and break all the rules ... but gets the job done.

Welcome to a new military romance series by *USA Today* best-selling author Dale Mayer. A series where you meet new friends and just might get to meet old ones too in this raw and compelling look at the men who keep us safe every day from the darkness where they operate—and live—in the shadows ... until someone special helps them step into the light.

Not the size to blend in anywhere ... Not that he cared ...

Beau heads to Alaska to a cult that kidnaps women to flesh out its numbers. One woman in particular has gone missing. When her father calls in a favor, Beau is asked to fit into the cult community. Only his style is guns blazing, and he doesn't bother counting the dead ...

Danica was late for her college class when a hood was thrown over her head, and then she was tossed into the back of a vehicle. Days later, she wakes up on a dirt floor of a cell with only a grate above her head. But she'll take it as she's nothing if not innovative. As soon as she escapes her prison, she runs into the brick wall that's Beau. He'd good at giving orders. She's not so good at following them …

With dozens of lives at stake in a sex-trafficking scheme, neither Beau nor Danica had expected it would be action all the way for them as they battle to free other women and to stay alive–together.

Find book 4 here!
To find out more visit Dale Mayer's website.
http://smarturl.it/DMBeauUniversal

Author's Note

Thank you for reading Jax: The Mavericks, Book 3! If you enjoyed the book, please take a moment and leave a short review.

Dear reader,

I love to hear from readers, and you can contact me at my website: www.dalemayer.com or at my Facebook author page. To be informed of new releases and special offers, sign up for my newsletter or follow me on BookBub. And if you are interested in joining Dale Mayer's Reader Group, here is the Facebook sign up page.
https://smarturl.it/DaleMayerFBGroup

Cheers,
Dale Mayer

Get THREE Free Books Now!

Have you met the SEALS of Honor?

SEALs of Honor Books 1, 2, and 3. Follow the stories of brave, badass warriors who serve their country with honor and love their women to the limits of life and death.

Read Mason, Hawk, and Dane right now for FREE.

Go here and tell me where to send them!
http://smarturl.it/EthanBofB

About the Author

Dale Mayer is a USA Today bestselling author best known for her Psychic Visions and Family Blood Ties series. Her contemporary romances are raw and full of passion and emotion (Second Chances, SKIN), her thrillers will keep you guessing (By Death series), and her romantic comedies will keep you giggling (It's a Dog's Life and Charmin Marvin Romantic Comedy series).

She honors the stories that come to her – and some of them are crazy and break all the rules and cross multiple genres!

To go with her fiction, she also writes nonfiction in many different fields with books available on resume writing, companion gardening and the US mortgage system. She has recently published her Career Essentials Series. All her books are available in print and ebook format.

Connect with Dale Mayer Online

Dale's Website – www.dalemayer.com
Facebook Personal – https://smarturl.it/DaleMayer
Instagram – https://smarturl.it/DaleMayerInstagram
BookBub – https://smarturl.it/DaleMayerBookbub
Facebook Fan Page – https://smarturl.it/DaleMayerFBFanPage
Goodreads – https://smarturl.it/DaleMayerGoodreads

Also by Dale Mayer

Published Adult Books:

Hathaway House
Aaron, Book 1
Brock, Book 2
Cole, Book 3
Denton, Book 4
Elliot, Book 5
Finn, Book 6
Gregory, Book 7

The K9 Files
Ethan, Book 1
Pierce, Book 2
Zane, Book 3
Blaze, Book 4
Lucas, Book 5
Parker, Book 6
Carter, Book 7

Lovely Lethal Gardens
Arsenic in the Azaleas, Book 1
Bones in the Begonias, Book 2
Corpse in the Carnations, Book 3
Daggers in the Dahlias, Book 4
Evidence in the Echinacea, Book 5
Footprints in the Ferns, Book 6

Gun in the Gardenias, Book 7
Handcuffs in the Heather, Book 8

Psychic Vision Series
Tuesday's Child
Hide 'n Go Seek
Maddy's Floor
Garden of Sorrow
Knock Knock…
Rare Find
Eyes to the Soul
Now You See Her
Shattered
Into the Abyss
Seeds of Malice
Eye of the Falcon
Itsy-Bitsy Spider
Unmasked
Deep Beneath
From the Ashes
Psychic Visions Books 1–3
Psychic Visions Books 4–6
Psychic Visions Books 7–9

By Death Series
Touched by Death
Haunted by Death
Chilled by Death
By Death Books 1–3

Broken Protocols – Romantic Comedy Series
Cat's Meow
Cat's Pajamas

Cat's Cradle
Cat's Claus
Broken Protocols 1-4

Broken and... Mending
Skin
Scars
Scales (of Justice)
Broken but... Mending 1-3

Glory
Genesis
Tori
Celeste
Glory Trilogy

Biker Blues
Morgan: Biker Blues, Volume 1
Cash: Biker Blues, Volume 2

SEALs of Honor
Mason: SEALs of Honor, Book 1
Hawk: SEALs of Honor, Book 2
Dane: SEALs of Honor, Book 3
Swede: SEALs of Honor, Book 4
Shadow: SEALs of Honor, Book 5
Cooper: SEALs of Honor, Book 6
Markus: SEALs of Honor, Book 7
Evan: SEALs of Honor, Book 8
Mason's Wish: SEALs of Honor, Book 9
Chase: SEALs of Honor, Book 10
Brett: SEALs of Honor, Book 11
Devlin: SEALs of Honor, Book 12

Easton: SEALs of Honor, Book 13
Ryder: SEALs of Honor, Book 14
Macklin: SEALs of Honor, Book 15
Corey: SEALs of Honor, Book 16
Warrick: SEALs of Honor, Book 17
Tanner: SEALs of Honor, Book 18
Jackson: SEALs of Honor, Book 19
Kanen: SEALs of Honor, Book 20
Nelson: SEALs of Honor, Book 21
Taylor: SEALs of Honor, Book 22
SEALs of Honor, Books 1–3
SEALs of Honor, Books 4–6
SEALs of Honor, Books 7–10
SEALs of Honor, Books 11–13
SEALs of Honor, Books 14–16
SEALs of Honor, Books 17–19

Heroes for Hire
Levi's Legend: Heroes for Hire, Book 1
Stone's Surrender: Heroes for Hire, Book 2
Merk's Mistake: Heroes for Hire, Book 3
Rhodes's Reward: Heroes for Hire, Book 4
Flynn's Firecracker: Heroes for Hire, Book 5
Logan's Light: Heroes for Hire, Book 6
Harrison's Heart: Heroes for Hire, Book 7
Saul's Sweetheart: Heroes for Hire, Book 8
Dakota's Delight: Heroes for Hire, Book 9
Michael's Mercy (Part of Sleeper SEAL Series)
Tyson's Treasure: Heroes for Hire, Book 10
Jace's Jewel: Heroes for Hire, Book 11
Rory's Rose: Heroes for Hire, Book 12
Brandon's Bliss: Heroes for Hire, Book 13

Liam's Lily: Heroes for Hire, Book 14
North's Nikki: Heroes for Hire, Book 15
Anders's Angel: Heroes for Hire, Book 16
Reyes's Raina: Heroes for Hire, Book 17
Dezi's Diamond: Heroes for Hire, Book 18
Vince's Vixen: Heroes for Hire, Book 19
Ice's Icing: Heroes for Hire, Book 20
Heroes for Hire, Books 1–3
Heroes for Hire, Books 4–6
Heroes for Hire, Books 7–9
Heroes for Hire, Books 10–12
Heroes for Hire, Books 13–15

SEALs of Steel
Badger: SEALs of Steel, Book 1
Erick: SEALs of Steel, Book 2
Cade: SEALs of Steel, Book 3
Talon: SEALs of Steel, Book 4
Laszlo: SEALs of Steel, Book 5
Geir: SEALs of Steel, Book 6
Jager: SEALs of Steel, Book 7
The Final Reveal: SEALs of Steel, Book 8
SEALs of Steel, Books 1–4
SEALs of Steel, Books 5–8
SEALs of Steel, Books 1–8

The Mavericks
Kerrick, Book 1
Griffin, Book 2
Jax, Book 3
Beau, Book 4
Asher, Book 5
Ryker, Book 6

Miles, Book 7
Nico, Book 8
Keane, Book 9
Lennox, Book 10
Gavin, Book 11
Shane, Book 12

Collections
Dare to Be You…
Dare to Love…
Dare to be Strong…
RomanceX3

Standalone Novellas
It's a Dog's Life
Riana's Revenge
Second Chances

Published Young Adult Books:

Family Blood Ties Series
Vampire in Denial
Vampire in Distress
Vampire in Design
Vampire in Deceit
Vampire in Defiance
Vampire in Conflict
Vampire in Chaos
Vampire in Crisis
Vampire in Control
Vampire in Charge
Family Blood Ties Set 1–3
Family Blood Ties Set 1–5

Family Blood Ties Set 4–6
Family Blood Ties Set 7–9
Sian's Solution, A Family Blood Ties Series Prequel Novelette

Design series
Dangerous Designs
Deadly Designs
Darkest Designs
Design Series Trilogy

Standalone
In Cassie's Corner
Gem Stone (a Gemma Stone Mystery)
Time Thieves

Published Non-Fiction Books:

Career Essentials
Career Essentials: The Résumé
Career Essentials: The Cover Letter
Career Essentials: The Interview
Career Essentials: 3 in 1

Made in the USA
Monee, IL
26 January 2020